In
Borrowed
Flesh

Laura Hughes

Chapter One

I am the thing that goes bump in the night; the movement you catch in the corner of your eye; the fear that keeps you awake because you sense me but aren't quite sure what I am. You feel me the way you feel a chill whose source you can't identify. The kind of chill that causes goosebumps to raise on your arms and makes you shiver uncontrollably. When I am near, the area around you becomes hushed and sounds strange to your own ears. The stillness in the air is uncomfortable; you feel as if you need to leave but don't know where to go because you aren't sure what you are running away from. Peering into a dimly lit room, you strain your eyes trying to catch a glimpse of the thing that's causing you discomfort, but you won't be able to see me. You might be able to see something like a mist that dissolves before you decide if you have seen anything at all. I, on the other hand, see far too much. It's frightening and disorienting.

It's dark where I am, but I can see you. You are very bright to my eyes. I think I still have eyes, but I'm judging by what I had when I was alive. I don't know what I am now but I'm sure I'm no longer living. It's weird for me to say that now because, to be honest, I don't feel dead. I have no solid form, but I am conscious of everything, just as I was before. I no longer have lungs that draw breath. No fingers to touch the physical world. No skin to feel the atmosphere around me. I'm now basically a shadow occupying space in the universe. Yet somehow, I still exist. I don't understand it, but on some level, I'm still something. A disembodied consciousness maybe? I hate to bring up the word "ghost" because I never believed in them when I was alive. It's funny what you remember about that part of your existence. In fact, one of the few things I do remember about my life before this is that I didn't believe in ghosts. I don't know my name, where I lived, or how old I was when I died, but I do remember not believing in supernatural things. Ghosts made for good stories around the campfire, and were great for a late-night movie on Halloween, but that was the extent of my experience with the floating sheet mentality.

My mind is often in a fog, but every once in a while, I have a flash of insight about who I might have been. People greeting me as I walked down some kind of school hallway. Faces smiling as they waved and patted me on the back. It seems I was popular and one of them. I sometimes see a locker that I opened and put books into. Geometry, Literature, History, generic titles giving no indication of the year they were published. There is no particular timeline to what I see. I often bounce from different stages of my life randomly, not seeing enough to give a decent clue as to what I'm witnessing. Short squatty limbs visible below me, running and kicking a ball, followed by a view of larger, pant-clad legs walking toward a big building. Attempting to get some clarity, I often try to force myself to stay in the moment, but the memories don't last long enough for me to figure out where I had been going or who I might have been. Sometimes I see my large hands working on pieces of metal and wood, painstakingly forming these items into decorative shapes whose purpose is unknown to me. Once in a while, I recognize car parts I seemed good at fixing; fingers leaving greasy smears on a cloth, before that picture faded away too. Other times I see a beautiful young woman walking by my side, smiling at me like I was the best thing she had ever seen before leaning in to kiss me. Then, just as suddenly, I see her crying and screaming, terror-filled eyes staring into mine. Horrified, I struggle to keep the vision going, to see more, but as hard as I tried, I can't. Memories tease me with their vagueness. I can't make them stay long enough to recall anything concrete about myself. Was I the reason she was so afraid? What kind of man could I have been to inspire that kind of reaction? Because that was the only thing I was certain of, that I was a man. A nameless, large man of questionable character who could have been a monster to those who loved him. Do I even want to know who I was? Sometimes I'm not sure. The possibility of who or what I may have been terrifies me. So here I am, a stranger even to myself. Wandering around in confusion, waiting for more visions to tell me what kind of life I lived; to justify my continued existence as a nameless shadow. If I could just figure out why I'm still here, wherever here is.

I don't even know where I am. Just that I seem to move quickly from place to place. The scenery around me changes often. I am in different rooms, watching different people, not certain how I made it there from the place I was before. I float around without any anchor to the real, solid world. I see things in shades of gray. There are no colors here. It's strange that I can talk to you now, but it's not my lips sharing the story. I speak through someone else. The telling of my tale is in no particular order. The timeline

4

is my own, having no way of putting it into relation to your time since it concerns only me.

First, I want to tell you about the woman. She was dead for a short time. I saw her walk into the fog, looking as confused as those who pop suddenly into the dense nothingness I move around in. My surroundings are like a smoke-filled corridor bordered by clearer areas that serve as windows to the living world. The few figures I encounter in my aimless wanderings are bland and blurry. The fresh ones are bright gray but quickly fade until I can't see them very well. They never speak to me, at least not in words I can hear. I get the impression of words that make no sense. The soul uttering them moves on quickly, not stopping to interact with me for more than a second. But this one time…I saw a burst of color and there she was, as clear and focused as a real person could be. She looked right at me and spoke, saying only three words. "Who are you?" before disappearing. I was so surprised by this turn of events, I felt compelled to find her. I followed the trail she left behind. It wasn't hard since it was a beautiful technicolor mist. Taunting me with its vibrancy, her essence encouraged me to pursue it to its destination. I zigged and zagged through the shadowy spaces, past many opaque windows leading to a world I used to be part of, until I found the one she had entered. And seeing no reason not to, I followed her through the opening. Her body was lying on a stretcher. There were two people in the process of reviving her. A big man was pushing on her chest as her light trail moved through the window into the living world, seeking out her body like a hungry animal seeks out fresh meat. "One, two, three, four, five," the man performing chest compressions was counting under his breath. "Come on, come on, lady; come back to us." After a few more aggressive repetitions, and with some kind of tube pushed into her side, she gasped and opened her eyes. I was pleased to note that she was looking right at me when she returned to life. Encouraged by this turn of events, I was determined to stay close and find out more about her. Contact had been made with a living person and I wasn't about to lose it. In fact, I was going to exploit it for all it was worth.

Chapter Two-Maddie

About the car accident that nearly took my life; well, all I can truly remember is that I swerved to miss a cow. Yes, a cow that had wandered into the road. I must have over-compensated because the next thing I knew I was bumping around in my car as it flipped upside down. An airbag exploded in my face; small projectiles from the interior thudded into me; change from the center console, some papers and books from the passenger seat, a jacket, my cell phone. I remember thinking, *oh crap, there goes my phone. How am I going to replace that? I don't have insurance on it.* Isn't that funny? A time like that and all I can think of is my cell phone. Well, I guess there is no standard rule as to what you should be thinking while undergoing a traumatic event. Anyway, sorry if I'm straying from the point. I do this when I'm stressed, okay? So, to continue; there I was tumbling around in my car, which as I now understand it, rolled over several times before coming to a stop, upside down. At this point, I knew nothing of this because the last roll crushed the roof, forcing my chest downward into the steering wheel, breaking some ribs, and puncturing a lung. It was sheer luck that the vehicle behind me happened to be an ambulance returning to the station. What are the odds of that happening? It must be a pretty rare occurrence because I've never heard of it before. Am I lucky or what! Sorry, I did it again. So back to the story. The two emergency workers inside the ambulance managed to get me out of the car. Sometime during that endeavor my heart actually stopped. Initially I felt the pain from every one of my injuries but when I died, it stopped immediately. In fact, I felt pretty good. I kinda already figured out what had happened the minute my soul left my body, because from high above, I could see one of the emergency guys thumping on my chest while the other one tried to force air into my lungs with a plastic bag. For a minute or two, I watched from over one of the guy's shoulder, wanting to tell him he was wasting his time. After all, I was obviously dead and, though I didn't want to be, didn't feel too bad about it. I know this makes no sense right now, but at the time I felt alright, a little sad about the people I was leaving behind, but not especially upset. You may not believe me, but I was more curious than scared. After watching the spectacle below for a second or two more, my spirit was pulled up and away by a tornado-strength wind. I found myself wandering around in a strange misty place. I guess this is where dead people go. I had no former experience with this kind of thing and didn't know the rules or layout of my new surroundings. I just hung there looking around in fascination, thinking I'd landed on a movie set, waiting for the lead character to emerge and say something really cool like *Welcome to the Afterworld, here's how everything works.* But after several minutes of nothing, it became obvious that there were no door greeters in the dead place and I decided to explore a bit.

The foggy area I was pulled into was mostly gray with lots of blurry forms that looked like people walking around. I couldn't really see their faces but passed many of them on my way towards a very bright light. I did try to stop and talk to some of them; all I got in response were garbled words. But judging by the tone of their voices, they were excited to see me. I mean, they were talking very fast with high-pitched, squeaky sounds coming from the direction of their heads,. One or two tried to follow me, reaching for me with icy cold fingers that couldn't quite grasp hold of my strangely warm blobby form. I plodded on towards the interesting, and oh so comforting light not far in front of me. The closer I got to the light, the more aggressively they grabbed at me. It was as if they did not want me to reach it. I picked up feelings of desperation and fear all mixed together as the shadowy forms continued to screech at me in some nonsensical language. Frankly, it was getting pretty scary. What had been intriguing was now a bit disturbing. Suddenly being dead didn't seem so wonderful anymore. The forms were quivering in and out of view while crowding around me aggressively. I know I had just arrived, but I didn't seem to blend in with them at all. Can they sense newbies?

From the scary movies I loved to watch, I had learned that ghosts usually have some kind of common bond with the living. But these ghosts didn't seem to like me. And the white light they say you should walk into seemed to be getting further away by the second. Not only that, but now there was a dark spot in front of it which felt cold and very unpleasant, making me back in the opposite direction. That's when I saw him standing behind me. While the other forms were blobs, this man appeared in grainy shades of gray like a character in an old black and white movie. I can't tell you what he was wearing or exactly how old he was, but his hair was short, his face smooth shaven, and he might have been wearing glasses. The man looked sad at first, then surprised to see me staring at him. I would have moved closer to introduce myself but there was a sudden popping sensation in my head. All I had time to say was, "Who are you?" before being pulled uncomfortably back into my body. My eyelids fluttered open. The big guy who brought me back to life was grinning at me with tears of relief in his eyes. As I came around, I was surprised to see the same gray man hanging over his shoulder, and knew at that moment that I would soon see more of him. For whatever reason, he was attached to me and wasn't going to go away until he told me why.

Chapter Three-Shadow Man

It was quiet for a while. I tried to stay with her all the time, even while she slept, watching and waiting for a chance to make contact. I could still see her clearly; a young woman with short dark hair. She wasn't skinny or fat, not stunning to look at, but not ugly either. Overall, she was a rather ordinary person with nothing to draw my attention, except she had been dead for a moment but had recovered. I stared at her until she woke up. I knew she could see me, especially after she re-entered her body and looked straight at me. But since the three words she had uttered in the dead place, she hadn't spoken to me and wouldn't acknowledge my presence. The thing about being dead, though; I had plenty of time on my hands and was determined to talk to her. I stayed close by, constantly saying things like, "I know you can hear me." I also asked her name, but she hadn't been left alone since she was brought back by Mr. Muscle Man and proceeded to ignore me. But the movement of her eyes as she tried to avoid looking at me, told me she was oh so aware that I was speaking to her. I could have kept up my assault on her senses, speaking non-stop until she gave in and said something back, but some sense of the human I used to be kicked in, and I realized this was the wrong approach. She wasn't likely to help me if I kept on this way. She had to be willing to let me in. I didn't have the experience to make her do what I wanted, but could perhaps connect with her if she would allow me to. Her brush with death made her enough like me to form a bond; a bond I wanted to use to its fullest extent, but it had to be voluntary. That bit of knowledge entered my mind with a certainty I couldn't ignore. Maybe it was a dead person thing. It was at that point that I just pulled back and watched, becoming again a heavy silence hanging in the background. I floated or stood near the portal she existed in, waiting for my opportunity to get through. Any sign she was receptive to me would do. I was afraid to move far, as my inexperience at navigating this dead place would make it hard to locate her again, so I kept her in my sights. As I waited for a chance, I began to sense a change in the atmosphere around me. Quick and hardly subtle, it felt like all the air had been sucked out of this space, leaving me in a vacuum. This sensation was more of a technique to get my attention than anything else because, being dead, I didn't need air. I hadn't encountered anything powerful enough to do this before. It made me wonder why and what had made it happen. The stillness that accompanied the change was intense and, ironically enough, I felt as if I were being watched. Was this some kind of cosmic turnabout for my behavior just a short while ago? If so, I didn't like it.

After wandering around in this vast nothingness, I was suddenly noticed. Whatever I was vibrated with the consistency of a charged atom, and if it were possible to be cold, I was now freezing. I didn't think at this point that anything could frighten me. After all, I had no physical form to protect. What could possibly happen to a dead man's spirit? I turned my sights behind me to look for the source of my discomfort. As I did, I saw a darkness so deep that despair radiated from its core, hovering directly behind me. It hung in the grayness, as a cloud so thick and black it nearly eclipsed the white column of light that appeared from time to time. I didn't like the light but didn't like the darkness either. The light showed itself to me many times, inviting me in with warmth and encouragement, but it made me uncomfortable. I avoided it each time it appeared. But the darkness was a new thing. I hadn't seen it before. It felt sick and ominous all at once. I liked it even less than the light. I don't know why it chose to show itself to me now, but the interest it took in me was disturbing. All I wanted to do was get away. But getting away would be difficult when this place was pretty much everything and everywhere with no defined boundaries. We hung there on opposite sides of the big empty void, me and my inky companion. I could hear its laughter in my head. A laughter that knew no joy; hollow and mirthless with promises of misery and endless suffering. The whole encounter was terrifying and over just as quickly as it started, ending with a sudden flare of the light which seemed to drive it away. After acting as my savior, the brightness beckoned me with its warmth, but I turned my back on it, moving as far away as I could in this vast expanse of nothingness. I hoped it would disappear and leave me alone. I desperately wanted it to go away. The noises that came from it hurt my heart because it sounded like children laughing, birds singing, and exclamations of sheer joy. Yet I chose to ignore all that, not wanting to accept what it promised. I didn't want to go in there. It wasn't where I belonged. There were too many unanswered questions about what I had been for me to be comfortable moving past my current state. After a few more minutes, in which it continued to offer me a chance to enter, it seemed to get the message that I was not coming and disappeared once again. Relieved at its absence, I continued to stare fixedly at the object of my interest. She was awake and alone now, a nurse having just left the room after telling her to push the call light if she needed anything. The nurse's last words to the woman were, "I'm glad you're doing better, Maddie," before the door closed behind her. Now I knew her name! I slid up next to her and whispered it into her ear, and for the first time since she died, she raised her head and answered me. "What!"

Chapter Four-Maddie

I was finally alone. Well, not really alone, he had never really left me. He had hung around the bed peering at me over the medical staff's shoulders with hopeful eyes, stalking me with his presence and constant conversation that I couldn't respond to. He followed me down the hallway as I walked with the physical therapist, trying to get my strength back; floating above the floor at my side whispering relentlessly in my ear. He had been there the entire time my mother and father sat at my bedside crying, talking to me every quiet moment, wanting me to acknowledge that he was there. I really did want to talk to him but doing so then would have made them run more tests on me to check for brain damage. And I must admit that while I was excited and curious about the possibility of communicating with this dead guy, he was getting a little bit annoying. I mean, do you know how much energy it takes to act like you're listening to the living people in front of you while ignoring the constant talking of someone no one else can see? Beside all that, I was tired and hurting a lot. It was finally beginning to sink in that I had actually died at the ripe old age of twenty-two, been brought back to life, and now a dead guy was following me around like we were married or something. Funnily enough, I had been married once, for a whole nine months to my high school sweetheart, but it wasn't all that great for me. Joe got into drugs and became a real jerk. After a long miserable time of soul-searching, of constant lectures from my parents, I divorced him. It was the best thing I ever did. Even though I had to live in a town filled with his resentful family members, I hadn't spent a minute regretting it. I could take a few dirty looks and whispers behind my back, especially since he was now in prison for selling drugs to an undercover cop. I'm sure his momma found a way to blame that on me too, even though we had been divorced for two years before that happened. It was always my fault. Even when he hit me and cheated on me. She had always hated me. And you know what's ironic? I was on my way out of town to make a fresh start, armed with a college degree in graphic arts and new job lined up. Because of a cow, here I am. Still stuck in this crappy little town with my parents and my hostile ex's family all around me, and now I have a ghost. *Okay, Maddie, slow down, get back on track; nerves again.*

Anyway, as I was saying, I'm sure divorce wouldn't make this guy go away. He seemed very determined to get my attention. When I first saw him, I'd been thrilled at all the possibilities of finding out what he might know and see from beyond this world, but the longer I was back in the land of the living, the less sure I was that it was such a good idea to talk to him. I mean, I'd seen movies about what could happen if you talked to dead people, and they weren't always good, were they? Sometimes they hurt you or the people you love when you didn't do what they wanted. When he started to bug me, I began to get more than a little bit suspicious. I had no idea who he was or used to be, but he was so persistent! What did he want from me, anyway? Did he have unfinished business in the world he needed help with; and what if he wasn't the only one? I hadn't seen much in that "other place", but plenty of things had seen me. What if one of those things that tried to talk to me had followed as well? Would I have to put up with more of them? I was beginning to get scared because one of those things was dark and very interested in me. I had felt it watching before I saw it. It was just a split second in time but the more I thought about it, the more I began to remember things that couldn't have happened. Flashes of something frightening that I may, or may not have experienced gnawed away at the back of my mind. Trying to recall it made my head hurt, and I shied away from exploring it further. None of this made sense. I hadn't been there long enough to have any significant encounters. I had been assured by Damen, the big guy who revived me, that I hadn't been dead all that long, only five minutes or so, and he was so happy to see me come back. He told me that he considered me one of his greatest successes, me being so young and tragically taken from this world by that damn cow. Damen has been to visit me often. I feel comfortable with him. I guess I'm flattered because he says he doesn't usually visit his patients like this; he seems genuinely interested in my well-being. He's funny and handsome and I look forward to him coming back. When he's here I feel safe and happy, but I also feel anger and frustration from my constant companion from the other side. To tell you the truth, I'm glad because I'm having serious second thoughts about talking to him again. Deep in thought, my fingertips tentatively touched the tube sticking out of my left side. it's one of the few things I haven't yet gotten rid of during my stay here. The doctor said I'm recovering, and it should be gone soon. The x-rays showed that my lung is almost working like it should, allowing me to be able to breathe normally again. I was lucky, really, because other than cuts and bruises, I have no permanent damage to my body. At this point, I'm more worried about my spiritual safety, as in staying safe from ghosts. I wish I'd paid closer attention to the movies I've watched, then I might have a clue how to protect myself from the spooky things like the one that attached itself to me. I wanted some kind of control in this new relationship, or whatever it was, that I had with this gray guy.

For the first time in a long time, I'd been awake and alone for a few minutes and hadn't heard or seen him. I still felt the strange emptiness that often accompanied him, but it was weaker than it had been before. I don't know where he was, but he wasn't as close as he had constantly been to this point. I was surprised because I expected him to appear next to me and start talking up a storm as soon as he had an opening, but nothing happened. It was blissfully silent. Wavering between disappointment and relief, I let out a deep breath and nearly jumped out of my skin when he suddenly appeared at my side, calling my name. I found myself speaking to him for the first time since I had seen him. "What?" And I knew I didn't sound eager or friendly.

He appeared taken aback. His grainy form lost shape for just a second before appearing more focused again. I say more focused, which is the same as saying he was more like a see-through cardboard cutout standing next to my bed. Other than his facial expression, there wasn't much movement to him; he was just a representation of human energy.

After a brief awkward pause, he gathered himself together and spoke. "I need you." The statement was simple and not what I expected after all the talking he'd done earlier. And if I wasn't mistaken, and I didn't think I was, I could've sworn he was a little bit afraid. He turned his head to the left a few times, looking back over his shoulder before turning back to me with a pleading expression.

"I don't know who I am, or why I'm here. You have to tell me who I am."

"How am I supposed to know that?" I blurted out. I mean, I wasn't trying to be a jerk but really, how was I supposed to react?

"Do you know your name?" I asked, trying to make up for what I had just said. Maybe this would be as easy as doing a little research and getting him to move on.

17

"I don't know who I am," he repeated as if I were a bit brain damaged, before glancing behind him once again. I found this a little bit disturbing as he had been so intent on getting me to understand him yet was concerned enough about something in that other place to move his focus away from me for a second or two.

"What do you keep looking at?" I asked, more interested in what was distracting him, forgetting I had been afraid of him and what he could potentially do to me. He was scared, my growing connection to him strangely conveying that from our great distance. He still hadn't answered the first question, when it occurred to me to ask him what could possibly frighten a dead person. That's when I had a brief flashback of an ugly dark cloud followed by a raspy voice saying something I couldn't quite understand. As I had this thought, he raised his head quickly. His eyes locked into mine and I knew, I just knew, that that is what he was afraid of. Without my ever having said a word, he was able to sense what I was thinking. Our bond was stronger than I realized.

"You saw it too?" he asked, fully aware that whatever we were sharing in this strange moment was the awareness of *It*.

"If by *It* you mean that dark thing in there, yes, I did, but there are a lot of other things in there too. I can't be sure exactly what I saw." His form wavered for a moment before flaring up again until I could see that I was speaking to a tall man in his twenties or thirties with glasses, not stunningly attractive, but not ugly either. His hair was dark, at least it was a darker shade of gray than his other features, and he was wearing a wrinkled, torn shirt and a pair of jeans covered in dark splotches that might have been blood.

"What happened to you?" I asked. It didn't look like he had gotten to where he was quietly and gently.

"I know even less about that then I know about myself," was his sad reply. We both sidestepped the issue neither of us were brave enough to broach at the moment, so the line of questioning centered just on him and what he needed.

"Okay." My voice filled the uncomfortable pause between us. "I'll help you, but it'll have to wait until I get out of here." I could tell he was less than satisfied with my answer. He frowned, not saying anything for a minute or two. If he wanted my help, he was going to have to do it my way, and I was going to have to learn how to do this correctly, whatever *this* was.

Trying to soften what I knew was a harsh response to his request, I continued with an explanation I hoped he would understand. "I can't talk to you while all these people are around. I'm sure they'd have a hard time letting me out of the hospital if I'm talking to myself like a crazy person." We shared another awkward silence. The temperature dropped, until I could see my breath in the air around me. Puffs of white escaped my lips as, shivering, I lay very still and waited for an answer to the conditions I set. The seconds ticked away, the television set high on the wall above me turned itself on and off several times before shutting off altogether. Once again, I had the nagging thought that maybe I wasn't making the best decision, but a feeling of desperation hung in the air around him; I could never resist helping an underdog. In the end, he merely nodded his head and disappeared into a fine mist. Though no longer visible, I could sense him lingering in the background as I closed my eyes and fell into an uneasy sleep.

Chapter Five-Shadow Man

She was going to help me. We had gotten that far. I felt a tremendous amount of relief and frustration at the same time. I wanted things to start now. I stayed around her, not completely satisfied with the condition that we wait until she got out of the hospital, but I did understand her point. Forced to bide my time and watch quietly once again, while she continued to move around with the living people, I remained silent. But the longer I had to stay quiet, the more frustrated I became, hanging around until she could talk to me. There were so many things I had to know, and though time wouldn't change the fact that I was dead, I was still partially in the nothingness waiting for the uncomfortable darkness to come back. Afraid to go far from her, and not thrilled to wait in the gray place, I stayed in her world for as long as I could, pulling energy from things around her. I could feel the hum of generated power coming from the machines close by. Drawn to it, I quickly discovered that pulling it into my essence made me stronger and able to linger here for an extended period of time. Fortunately, there was plenty of electrical equipment for me to choose from, but my needs had a profound effect on the things I used. They had to replace the fluid pumps in her room so often that when she no longer needed intravenous antibiotics, they removed them completely. Eventually, because blood pressure machines and other electric devices had an odd habit of becoming completely drained not long after having been used on her, the staff had noticed and begun to talk about it, making her the center of unwanted attention. From the look she gave in my general direction, when she did acknowledge me at all, I knew I had to back off. I was making her stand out and not in a good way. So I pulled back, keeping my distance until I found myself once again in the doorway between our worlds, glancing behind me nervously for the presence I knew was waiting there. I had spent so much time in the land of the living, I was surprised it hadn't moved on. But, even though I couldn't see it, I knew it was still there; it would always be there. I had been in the doorway for a short while, though to tell you the truth, it's hard for me to tell how time passes here, and I was very uncomfortable. When I was watching her in the world of the living, I could keep up with time by looking at the clocks, before I sucked all the juice out of them, that is. And the nurses would write the date on a board in the room, so I knew when the days changed. But when I had to leave, I felt lost again. All that grounded me was in the living world with her. I was on the outside but wished I wasn't. My insubstantial form was even more insubstantial in the dead space. I was simply a shimmering white form much like an image on a badly tuned television station; at least that's what my hand looked like when I glanced down at it. Damn her for making me stay in here! I had had a brief taste of life again when I was with her and resented not having it even more now that I wasn't part of it. I was an anonymous nobody, not even having a name to call myself. I had the feeling that if I just knew something about my past, I would know what to do next. The more I thought about it, the more I became convinced that Maddie was my way out, the answer to all my questions. I just had to get back in there and make her help me. As soon as this thought, this resolution, came to me, I knew I was not alone. The atmosphere around me vibrated with an energy that once again indicated *It* was here and this time closer than ever before. Choking back a fear that was primal and not at all keeping with my immortal existence, I moved as far away from the darkness as I could. But it didn't seem to make any difference. *It* followed me closely, as if already aware of what I was doing and determined to stay with me. *It* was everywhere, streaming through the air first on one side of me, then the other, chasing me. I panicked, forgetting for a second that I was supposed to be staying close to Maddie, moving away from the window to her world as fast as I could. Seeking only to get away from the ill-feeling thing that was intent on overtaking me, I sped through the bleakness passing blurry figures who seemed to dissolve into a mist. They would be no help, no refuge, even though I knew they were aware of me. In my headlong flight to nowhere, I passed through one of my anonymous companions; that's when I had my first substantial encounter with anything besides the darkness. The young blonde woman was clearly visible to me when I moved through her essence. I got the impression of strong perfume and a face that had attracted plenty of admirers. With full lips and high cheek-bones, she was stunning, looking all of about twenty-five when she left the world. I was shown who and what she had been. Vivid green eyes stared at me when the spirit presented herself as she had appeared while still alive. In our split-second encounter, I saw her life pass before my eyes and knew more about her than I knew about myself. She had many amorous encounters during her lifetime, all the men she shared herself with thought she was gorgeous but stupid and desperate. It seemed that she was aware of this. As a result, she tried even harder to gain their acceptance, to the point of making a public spectacle of herself. I could see her talking too loudly, interrupting conversations she didn't understand to impress the man she was with, calling too often, showing up spontaneously just to make sure they were alone and not with another woman. Despite less than enthusiastic reactions, she tried even harder to gain approval from her companions by dressing in things that were embarrassing to wear anywhere but in a strip club, giving gifts she couldn't afford in order to buy affection, and doing any undignified thing asked of her. But rather than receiving genuine love for all her hard work, she was used and cast aside over and over again. She moved from man to man, hoping that with each new relationship she would find the one who would sweep her off her feet and give her the happily-ever-after life she longed for. It wasn't until the last few hours of her life, alone in a rented apartment, settling into a warm bathtub with an entire bottle of sleeping pills dissolving in her stomach, that it occurred to her, maybe she should have been a little nicer to herself. She had never really loved herself and so no one else had either. This was all so clear at the time when she found it hard to stay awake. Saying a silent goodbye to the three children she had aborted, and the one now living with a nice family in upstate New York, she slipped into unconsciousness. The woman was vaguely aware of her body sliding into the ceramic tub, head dipping under the water, but was too physically and emotionally exhausted to fight for life when the last breath escaped as bubbles from her lips. The feminine presence watched the bubbles pop on the liquid surface while she rose above her lifeless form resting at the bottom of the tub. From high above it all, she felt a little sadness, noting only that she was still very pretty, even in death. With one last glance at her lovely dead body, she sped away only to find herself moving among a bunch of shady blobs in a grainy, gray place. And now, after what seemed like forever, she sensed me and lovingly caressed my face, doing what she remembered doing when she was alive. Old habits die hard, I guess. Being a man, I might have been enthusiastic about all the attention when I had a body but now this just didn't feel right. I heard her whisper into my ear, "Now that you're here, maybe I can go with you instead of that awfully bright light. You're lonely, aren't you? I know I am." I got the impression of her name, Jeannie, along with visions of what she might do for me if I would just stay with her. Even in death, she was clingy and needy; clearly loss of life had not changed her personality. The clarity of her final moments had faded away into the familiarity of her former self. Rather than feeling flattered or aroused in any way, I felt pity and disgust. Was this what we were, remnants of our best and worst characteristics? She seemed stuck in her role as a desperate, lonely woman. Forgetting for a second that I was afraid of the thing that was chasing me around, I fought to separate myself from this suffocating, emotion-draining soul. With a desperate wrenching motion, I pulled away. Cries of "Don't leave me!" sounded loudly in my head. I glanced nervously about the echoing void for the ill-feeling mist I had been running from. It was nowhere in sight. Not sure what this meant, I moved cautiously, expecting to see it any second. I wasn't sure how long a second would have been here but I was ready to run for it once again as soon as I sensed it anywhere close to me. There I was, in the dull, continuous stretch of nothing, watching groups of spirits flit past me while moving away from the glistening mist I now knew as Jeannie. She tried to stay with me for a while but I moved faster, losing her in another section of wherever I was. When I was finally able to slow down and feel relieved at having evaded both of my worrisome pursuers, I stopped abruptly. I realized that I didn't know where I was. I was now far from Maddie's window, just as lost as I'd been before I found her.

Chapter Six-Maddie

It was amazingly quiet in my head. It had been weeks since dead guy had spoken to me. I didn't know what else to call him since he didn't know his name, and I hadn't had a chance to think one up for him. In the time of silence, a lot of things had happened. My new employers called and told me I no longer had the job; I had apparently taken too much time to heal, but they would certainly keep me in mind for the next available opening. I left the hospital a few days later without a chest tube and ironically enough, in good enough shape to get in my car and leave town for the job that no longer existed. Damen, having become very attached to me, continued to visit while I stayed with my parents and decided what I was going to do next.

That first ride in a car after the accident was quite an adventure. I found it hard not to flinch at every bump and dip in the road as Damen, driving carefully as he could, took me home, and got me settled in my childhood room. He awkwardly placed a kiss on my forehead and patted my arm with shaky hands. I knew he was trying to pretend he was still just my friend, interested only in supporting me, though I knew he felt more. But with all that had happened recently, he was holding back and I, being preoccupied with the expectation of my un-living companion making a surprise visit at any time, wasn't in any position to encourage him. I touched his handsome face and let him go on his way with a promise to call him soon. Only I wasn't sure I would. I was beginning to care a bit too much about him. As I watched him walk to the door, his lovely six-foot frame treading carefully on my mother's clean carpet, apologizing to her for almost knocking over her imitation Chinese vase located too close to the entryway; I had to choke back tears because I wasn't sure I could include him in this situation. That first day in the house I sat through dinner with my parents, on pins and needles, waiting for dead guy to contact me. I knew he had been watching and as soon as he could, would try get through, but I had to be alone. I had made that clear to him. I couldn't be seen talking to nothing. On one hand, I was the heroine in a paranormal mystery, just like those great movies I had always enjoyed. On the other, my original enthusiasm had dampened a bit when realizing that there were certain risks associated with dealing with the dead. I was still intrigued by this whole thing and the possibility of finding out more about that place I had been, but there was fear also, because a few days ago the dreams had started. Night after night, the darkness had visited me. At first, it just hovered close to my head. I was asleep but could see it as clearly as if I was awake. I believe it was really there, passing as easily through the thin layer of nothing as that other guy, more easily, in fact, and that worried me because I sensed it had more strength and was very angry. At first, it only stayed there, letting me know I had gotten its attention, but then it tried to talk to me. I often woke up in a panic, sweating and shaking as I struggled to remember what the garbled voice had been saying. This had happened so often I was afraid to sleep. Naps were out of the question; a full night's sleep was just as difficult. As a result, rather than recovering in the relatively peaceful atmosphere of my parents' home, I looked and felt worse than the entire time I spent in the hospital. Mom and Dad were worried. They encouraged me to rest, and discussed my return to the hospital if this continued. I stayed away from them as much as possible, and pretended every time I saw them that I was doing what I was supposed to, all the while wishing that I still had the privacy afforded by living in my own apartment. But, until I could get my life back together, I had to stay here and find out what was happening. Maybe my dead friend would be able to help me, so I waited for him, but he didn't show. I knew he needed to talk to me as much as I now needed to talk to him. Each quiet moment I spent waiting for him to appear was an eternity. Here I am pacing back and forth in my room, not knowing exactly what to do, but sure I need to do something.

When I had first come back to my childhood room, I had unpacked all the books I had collected on ghosts and hauntings, poring over them for any experiences like mine. But, other than the standard brief periods of contact with a spirit, the writers of the stories did not describe a situation anything like this. I had done some research on my computer, too unsure of myself to contact anyone for advice. This was too personal, too crazy for me to admit to another person just yet. And really, I didn't want to share this with anyone and was determined to handle it on my own, just like I had everything else in my life. I struggled to keep my eyes open, fighting the exhaustion that had threatened to take me over, I tried valiantly to stay awake. Looking around, I whispered softly to the empty places around me. "Where are you?" The silence continued, stretching on until my head throbbed and dizziness overtook me.

Exhausted now, I was forced to take a seat on my bed or fall to the floor; I couldn't give in to sleep. I needed a distraction, something to keep me awake. So, reaching for my remote I turned on my television, and what do you know, one of my favorite shows was on. The blood red letters of the title swam onto the screen *Meeting and Greeting Ghosts with Herbert Delmont*. Sitting up as straight as my droopy, tired body would allow, I watched the latest episode enrapt, hoping to learn something that would help me deal with my current situation. The dashing tall ghost-hunting expert appeared on the screen, strutting confidently toward an imposing-looking building on a hill above him. Dramatic music played in the background as Mr. Delmont explained his latest mission. It seemed this particular building was known as the Ferber building, built in eighteen ninety-five by wealthy businessman Cecil Ferber for his lovely young wife Elissa. My tired mind hit pause for a second as I processed the fact that this story sounded a little bit like an episode I watched two weeks ago, only the names of those involved were different. In fact, it seemed I remembered other shows with the same general theme; I guess there were a lot of old rich guys building houses for younger women. It's odd how I never gave that a thought before.

Shaking my head at the return of my ramblings, I tried to focus my attention to the program playing out in front of me. Herbert was talking about contacting and removing a vengeful ghost from the property, so the newest owners could fulfill their dream of making it a profitable bed and breakfast. It seemed that a horrible thing had happened in that house after Cecil had settled his young wife there and gone off on many business trips leaving her for long periods of time. Apparently, leaving her alone was not a good idea, because it wasn't too long before she found someone younger and better-looking to keep her company. Long story short, Cecil came home one day to find Elissa entertaining her new friend in a very unladylike fashion, and killed them both in a jealous rage, before hanging himself in the front hall. The unfortunate couple was hacked to death in a frenzied manner that had shocked local law enforcement at the time. Since then, the house had been occupied only sporadically, with each owner leaving months after taking possession of the property. Strange noises, cold spots, objects being moved, and foul odors were all common complaints by those who stayed in the house for any period of time. It had gotten so uncomfortable for the newest owners, who were attempting to convert it into a profitable business, that they called in an expert to solve their problem and draw national attention to their establishment - none other than television personality Herbert Delmont. The intrepid ghost hunter, psychic, medium, exorcism specialist was going to spend the night in the reportedly haunted mansion, accompanied by his trusty cameraman Neil and supernatural-detecting equipment operator Shaun. My eyelids were sagging over bloodshot eyes when something he said during the séance caught my attention. "There is a darkness that wants to come through. I see it lingering just beyond the portal of this world. I feel its hatred. It speaks to me in garbled tongue, I can't understand it but know it's not a good thing."

My eyes were wide open now, staring at Herbert. He was sitting at a table holding hands with Neil, Shaun, two blonde-haired women, and a dark-haired man. After a sudden dramatic silence, the supernatural television star looked in the direction of the camera with glassy, unfocused eyes, and began speaking in a squeaky voice that sounded vaguely familiar. At first, it was slow and unsteady, just like the voice of the thing that had been speaking to me, then its pitch increased and evened out after an edited minute during which Shaun's voice narrated:

"Herbert's body has been occupied by a spirit. This is not the first time this has happened. Don't worry, he knows how to handle himself." Shaun's thin, bearded face looked serious but confident as he spoke directly into the camera. "We have encountered darkness before. It's usually a very angry spirit in search of revenge. These entities tend to attach themselves to places or people that can help them resolve their issues. They can only affect change for themselves if they have a person to use; otherwise they just make life miserable for those around them."

Spooky music played in the background as I considered what I'd heard. Was the darkness contacting me because it had something to tell me, something it wanted me to do, just like nameless guy? This show really was useful! Herbert continued to sit at the table, his eyes wide, eyebrows dramatically raised as he continued to speak in words no one could understand. I was to change channels, because, though it was in the middle of the afternoon, it was over twenty-four hours past my bedtime, and I was still afraid to go to sleep. My tormentor had no hourly restrictions and I didn't want to face it again. As much as I wanted to find out what Herbert had to say, I couldn't spare much more of my wakeful time on something I couldn't understand. Trembling finger poised above the arrow button that would change the channel, further delaying slipping into dreamland, I waited impatiently for some kind of important revelation from the illustrious Mr. Delmont, something I could use as a defense against all this otherworldly company. My eyelids fluttered,, dragging me into impending slumber, the darkness I had been dreading all day. Only for Herbert to suddenly speak in a clear, gruff voice, saying something I hadn't expected to hear: my name followed by a warning.

Chapter Seven-Shadow Man

I was wandering again, speeding past several dirty windows into the living world. It then occurred to me that maybe I could reach out to another person, making this all easier than it currently was. There were many people present in the places I passed; a young man sitting all by himself in a room reading seemed a likely target to approach, as there was no one around to witness our encounter. Despite my doubts about his suitability and the dull, uninviting color of his energy, I decided to give him a try and passed through the filmy material separating me from him. Moving closer, I made the room as cold as I could, but he merely rubbed his arms and continued reading. Whispering in his ear did no good either. Shaking his head, he just turned up the radio that had been playing softly from the table next to him and resumed perusing the dirty magazine in his lap. Apparently, naked women were far more interesting than the possibility of a supernatural encounter. He was firmly planted in his own erotic reality and not open to listening to anything other than his own heavy breathing. Some people were rooted in the living world and their tiny, blinkered role in it to pick up anything else. Disgusted, I moved back into the gray space and continued searching the light-colored areas for anyone else that might detect my presence. Maybe it would be easier to find another person like Maddie than to hope I could find *her* again. There had to be someone else like her, someone I could get through to and use in the same way. I just had to keep looking for the colors that accompanied a person who was connected to both the living and dead worlds. She couldn't be the only one who had ever had this happen, there must be more. With this possibility to spur me on, I slid along on strands of air, flitting from area to area, spying on residents, trying to make contact of some kind.

The living went about their daily rituals in a closed fashion, not caring about anything other than their own worlds, especially when surrounded by other living people. Keeping that in mind, I avoided each person who was not alone. Scene after idyllic scene was shown to me as I witnessed people preparing meals in ordinary kitchens, watching television with family, celebrating birthdays with friends. All these situations were too busy, far from the perfect way to connect with someone. I wanted only certain contact with a willing soul, and found it in the fifteenth opening I came upon after leaving the lusty lad with his fantasy magazine. There was something different about the room I saw beyond the veil separating me from that place. This room had an aura about it that drew me in. I felt and smelled something so familiar that I was pulled toward it by a force I couldn't have resisted if I tried. The odor was sharply metallic and sweet at the same time, having no nose I can only explain that I knew it from something I experienced in my past. This scent triggered feelings that alarmed me, fear burrowed itself deep into my soul. Drifting into the room like a plume of gray smoke, I explored my surroundings to reason out my unexplained reaction to it. At first, all I could see was a total mess; chairs turned on their sides, cushions from a blue and gold couch strewn around the room. A tall table lamp with its base cracked and wires exposed, flickered on and off, giving the appearance of an invasion of fireflies. As I hung close to the floor in the form of a shadow, I noticed a red substance trickling across the wooden surface. My eyes followed the crimson trail to its source, while I listened to something that sounded like a wet towel being slapped against a concrete floor. Though it took me a minute to focus, I was soon able to understand what was going on around me.

I witnessed an event that was meant to be carried out in secret, one that shared a bizarre intimacy between two people, hardly equal or voluntarily on the part of the participants. What I saw was murder. There was nothing I could do to stop this encounter, only watch as splash after splash of red stuff was flung across the room while a knife entered the body of an old woman. The attacker, whose face was covered with a dark ski-mask, showed no signs of stopping his gruesome task, even though he had stabbed her so many times she was clearly not going to survive. Large beefy arms pinned her thin body down. He grunted with exertion from his activity. Force was no longer necessary, as it seemed the woman didn't have the strength to fight back. Wet pieces of cloth clung to her skin, forced into her wounds by the impact of the weapon. Her eyes were unfocused and glassy. Soft gasps filled the air while the last of this woman's life left her body and a gray mist rose up to look at what was being done to it. With an anguished expression, she then sensed me; I guess because we were now both officially dead. She looked straight at me, began to speak.

"Can't you make him stop?" she said sadly as the man continued to slash at her unmoving body. "He's already made quite a mess of me. How are my children going to be able to view my body at the funeral if it's all slashed up?" Her insubstantial form tried to reach for the man's head but was unable to do so. I continued to watch as a fascinated bystander, feelings of muted alarm and disgust flooding through me. I listened to the sloshing sound of metal meeting flesh, while flashes of violence from another time and place moved through my mind. Blood, screaming and the impression of pain, I just couldn't pin it down. I didn't want to deal with this woman's issues, I wanted to figure out why this situation was affecting me so strongly. Another sharp command from the old woman shook me out of my musing. "Stop him!"

Her see-through body gestured wildly from her attacker to me and I was treated to the full force of her anger. Though newly dead, she had enough rage to transmit itself to me. Her first and only thought was to make me do what she asked. She launched herself in my direction. Her mist moved through me quickly, her aura mingling with mine until all I wanted was desperately to get this fat man off my, I mean her, body.

"Get out!" I yelled, basically at myself because she was firmly entwined in my essence, clinging to it with ferocious tenacity born of desperation and anger.

"Make him stop!" she yelled back from inside the swirling mist that was now comprised of both of us. I just wanted the old woman to leave. I wasn't particularly kind enough to do this out of the goodness of my heart; unsure if kindness was a trait I had even possessed. I thought for a second about my ability to control something in the solid world, anything I could use to do what she asked of me, so I could make her leave. Remembering my connection with electrical things, I channeled all my energy toward a chandelier hanging from the ceiling. Instead of drawing power from the object as I had in Maddie's presence, I sent out a little of whatever made up my essence. The next thing I knew, light bulbs began to explode, showering the scene below in shards of glass, startling the killer enough to make him stop stabbing the woman's body. Cursing, he rose and swiped at his arm, picking out pieces of broken light bulb that had pierced his skin. Then, having determined his victim was dead, proceeded to move about the house, stripping cases off pillows and loading them with anything he thought could be sold, destroying whatever was of no use to him.

I watched a little longer while the murderous man pulled the fabric mask off his fat face, flung it aside and continued his passage through the dead lady's home. Having done what I could, I evicted her soul from my body, and moved toward the slim opening I had wandered in from, quickly exiting with her enraged cries following me.

"He's stealing my stuff, my children's stuff. Make him stop!"

Free from my obligation to her, I moved on. She stayed where she was, screaming at the murderous burglar who couldn't see her. I was glad she was so preoccupied that she didn't think to follow me. I didn't think I could handle another pitiful spirit attaching itself to me. I had enough problems of my own without adding her burden to them. Happily leaving her behind, I soared into the nothingness in search of something I would recognize, some place in which I could find a reason I still existed.

I flung myself about the dreary nothingness for a while longer, avoiding most windows into the living places until by sheer chance I saw it again, a faint colored light standing out among the blandness. It was Maddie! I headed eagerly toward the colorful display leading to the lighted opening she dwelled in. I was almost there, could feel the connection between us once again; it called to me, welcoming me back with warm familiarity. Approaching it with eagerness and relief, I noticed something distressing: a dark cloud heading for the same place. Slowing to an indecisive halt, I watched the swirling mass, which either didn't notice or didn't care that I was there, hover outside the entrance of her world. It had found her, and I was worried. She was mine. I had discovered her first and this thing was interested in her too. While I was afraid of this thing, I was also very angry that it was latching onto my living person; the one human I was counting on to answer all the questions I had about myself. I watched in dismay as the thing stayed a second or two more before moving on to another opening a short way down from hers. With a sigh of relief, I moved once again to her place in the world.

Chapter Eight-Maddie

With eyelids so heavy that I could barely focus, I watched Herbert's lips move. Amid the jumble of incomprehensible words he spits out, my name was suddenly very clearly spoken. In case I had mistaken what I just heard, he said it again, "Maddie."

To further clarify that it wasn't some other Maddie from the history of the house, he said my entire name. "Maddie Shorn." Herbert Delmont's face turned toward the camera and delivered the message he had been possessed to give to me.

"Maddie Shorn," the squeaky voice passed through its spokesperson. "Do not trust him. He is not what he seems!" I looked on in disbelief as my name was broadcast on national television, and hoped that no one I knew was watching. I liked to stand out occasionally, but this would not be the way I would want to be known. The only thing that would be worse was if my exact location was included along with everything else. The amazed looks of Herbert's companions, Shaun and Neil, had me panicking; maybe they would do some of their famous in-depth investigations and find me. Then I would have a lot of explaining to do. I didn't want to be known as the girl who could talk to dead people! This kind of fame would make me look stupid and dramatically reduce my ability to get a reputable job. I would be seen as a freak. The only way I could make a living would be to be on one of those *reality* shows where I had to share astonishing information with the living from their deceased family members. I could see my life after that; people would laugh at me, or I'd be followed by all kinds of weird groupies. All of this because I'd been in a stupid car accident and died for a few minutes! A bleak future played out in my head as I tried to figure out how to sneak out of town, change my name, and keep dead people away from me. Scenario after scenario was considered only to be discarded by the full impact of the voice's message. As usual, my imagination was running away with me and totally missing the point. What was that he said about not trusting him? Was the *him* my dead guy? Since I didn't really know who or what he was, I hadn't quite developed any trust yet. In fact, I was still very much undecided as to what I was going to do. And the darkness hardly inspired trust on my part; it scared me quite a bit. I was so tired I couldn't be sure anything I had seen or heard was real. I didn't know what to think. I had to get up and walk around to clear my head while Herbert Delmont continued to babble about something else in a woman's voice, something about how her husband had killed her. There was nothing more about me and who I wasn't supposed to trust. As I continued to fret, I noticed something else quite interesting; I wasn't even awake and so couldn't be quite sure if anything I heard had even happened. I discovered this astonishing fact when I attempted to rise from the floor and found myself looking down at my own body. This unexpected incident reminded me of the time I had died. Only this time, I was breathing and looking like I had passed out from an all-night drinking spree. Wow, was I ugly!! My hair was sticking up all over the place and there was drool on the pillow I had propped up under my head. There were lines under my eyes, and I realized why my parents had been so concerned. Having consciously avoided mirrors for days now, I couldn't believe that Damen had looked at me so adoringly on his last visit. I was horribly embarrassed and decided I would have to do something about this as soon as I could. Recalling my resolution to not see him again, I regretted that this would be how he remembered me.

And then, in the midst of all my superficial worrying, it hit me. I was observing myself from a distance while still alive. The scary thing wasn't bothering me, and I was moving around without my body. Needless to say, this incident scared me more than dying had. I wasn't sure how this was happening. Having had no experience with this, and being uncertain how to proceed, I hung above my body trying to figure out why this was happening. Whatever I was now took a moment to look around the room. The television was still on, playing the closing credits of Mr. Delmont's program. Daylight bathed my body and the surrounding area in its golden light. I was alone, with no sign of the darkness anywhere around me. I could see the whole of the room quite easily. I guess exhaustion had loosened up my inhibitions and tapped into something I had experienced while dead. I'm sure I wouldn't have been able to figure this out if I had continued to fight sleep, so maybe this was a good thing. I continued to cautiously look around the room, expecting the bad thing to try and speak to me again at any second. My actions were conscious, unlike my body which was still obviously asleep. This was definitely an interesting development, one I would have to explore further another time. An inner sense that something was happening around me necessitated a return to my body. A slight shifting in the air, followed by a flare of white in the left corner of my room, caused me to float quickly back down to my sleeping form and slip back inside. I almost didn't make it in time. Another form hovered over me, studying me closely as I slept. I don't know how I knew that because I really was still asleep, but he was there, my dead guy. My mind was as active now as if I had just had twenty-four hours of sleep and had taken adrenaline on top of that. And all that awareness was followed by nothing, because as quickly as the rush hit me, it left. I fell back into a deep sleep with the knowledge that he was waiting for me to wake up.

Chapter Nine-Shadow Man

After all I had been through to find her, it was irritating to see that she was asleep, yet again. Nothing I did to wake her up was working. Whispering in her ear. Knocking things off her shelves with gusts of energy generated from her radio. I knew she was alone in the house. The energy her parents put out was absent, so I didn't bother to be quiet with my efforts to get her lazy butt up. But no matter what I did, she just lay there with her mouth open, snoring softly. I didn't know how long I had been gone but, judging by the mess her room was in - before I messed it up even more - she must have been home for a while. She looked awful. For all I knew, she'd taken to drinking and hanging out in her room all the time. There were food wrappers on the floor, and though I didn't see any liquor bottles, she certainly looked as if she had passed out on the floor for some reason. Maybe I had connected with the wrong person, but I now considered her my person, and I would just have to make her acceptable. So, I waited - albeit impatiently - for her to wake up. I didn't know what time it was when she did wake, but the sun had set and risen again before her majesty roused herself. I was a little bit surprised when she looked up at me like she expected I would be there. She didn't appear the least bit shocked that I was hovering above her. In fact, she just stood up and said, "What took you so long?" before walking to the adjoining bathroom on heavy feet, throwing a, "Don't you dare follow me!" over her shoulder.

Peeved at her attitude, I knocked over a row of books on her dresser, stopping when I realized I was using up the valuable energy keeping me here. Hanging lamely in mid-air, I waited through the sound of the toilet flushing and then, to my annoyance, the hiss of running water from the shower. After tarrying in the bathroom, she finally emerged with a towel wrapped around her head and fluffy blue robe belted firmly in place.

"Now, Perry," she said. I was sure she was referring to me, looking straight at me when she said it.

"Who's Perry?" My curiosity was piqued. "Did you find out something about me while I was gone?" Maybe she had been doing something, after all. The name didn't sound familiar, but maybe if she told me more, it would come to me. I tried not to show my excitement at the possibility of finally learning who or what I was, trying to ignore the nagging dread that came with that same knowledge.

"Perry, was my first dog," she said casually, sitting on the bed, and talking to me as if I should have found that funny. Irritated, I shattered the bulb in the lamp next to her bed. She shrieked and jumped up, showing a look of first fear, and then anger.

"Do that again and I won't help you," Maddie said, looking me straight in the eye without moving another inch.

Shifting my shape to appear as menacing as I could, I hung before her as a wavering mist, making the room so cold I could see the breath coming from her lips. Rubbing her arms, she simply pulled the cover from the bed and wrapped it around her.

"Do you think this is a joke?" I whispered in her ear, letting her feel the anger boiling up inside me. Each word released with a hiss that moved the hair escaping the towel on her head. Her jaw shivered for a moment before she clamped her lips together and refused to speak or even look at me. If I could have shaken her I would have, but I hadn't figured out how that would be possible. It wouldn't help my situation to hurt her, but at this moment I was almost angry enough to try. My energy was quivering both with this knowledge and the way it made me feel; strong, invincible, and good to be feared. Bothered beyond imagining by this, I hung close for a moment more before moving to the other side of the room to gather myself together. I needed her more than I was willing to let her know, and couldn't afford to alienate her like this.

Shaking her head and closing her eyes, Maddie spoke again with great effort. "No, I do not!" she snapped at me tightly, as if controlling the movement of her mouth was difficult. "I'm merely trying to find a way to communicate with you and chose the name of something I was fond of to identify you." With the distance between us having gotten greater, she was able to open her eyes and look across the room at the shadowy form I had assumed to save energy.

"I wasn't trying to be funny," she repeated, her tone sincere and apologetic. Encouraged by my silence, she continued to explain. "I haven't slept well lately, and it was the first thing I thought of." I waited for a second to hear why she wasn't sleeping, but she didn't elaborate. I had the feeling she was leaving something out of her explanation and wanted her to tell me what she was hiding but knew I'd get no further confidences after what I'd just done.

I would have to pay closer attention to what she did from now on. I wasn't sure how long I had been gone but something about her was a little different, she seemed less trusting than when we first met. Not that she hadn't started to set rules before, but she had been eager to help and was more in awe of me than she was now.

"Can we start again?" I asked. Deliberately keeping my voice low and calm, I offered an apology and tried to explain my actions. "I got lost in the dead place and had a hard time finding my way back to you. I'm sorry I broke your lamp and knocked your stuff over. I promise I won't do that again." Shifting into my more human-looking form, I smiled at her sheepishly. "Will you help me?" I asked with the sweetest tone I could muster. I had a feeling I'd been quite charming when it suited me in my lifetime. The thought came to me from nowhere, part of the tantalizing yet insignificant flashes I occasionally got. Not my name, where I lived, or how I died, just that I could be quite charming when I wanted to. I knew that alone I didn't stand a chance of discovering anything significant about myself; I needed her help.

Maddie was silent for a moment, looking at me solemnly while she considered my plea. Though she was shaken by my earlier behavior, I could tell she was intrigued by the idea of helping solve my mystery and, of course, talking to a dead guy. As much trouble as I had been to her from the beginning, I could tell she wanted to have this experience. If she had not been, she wouldn't have put up with me for this long.

The books I knocked over all had sensationalized titles including the words *ghosts* and *hauntings*. Their worn appearance told me a lot about her interests, and here I was, a real ghost for her to communicate with. I waited in silence for the answer I was sure she would give. She nodded her head. Greatly encouraged, I was ready to begin finding out all I could about myself; she just had to start, somehow.

I watched expectantly as she rose from her bed and walked across the room to pick up the books I'd thrown there. Placing them carefully on a small desk, she slid a thin notebook out from among them, flipped through unlined pages until she found one that wasn't covered with drawings. Grabbing a pencil off the floor, she looked at me once again and began to sketch my form.

"What are you doing?" I tried to keep my tone merely curious and not show the mounting frustration and anger I was beginning to feel.

"In order to find out who you are, I need to know who to look for." Looking up from her task with raised eyebrows she spoke again, "Unless you have anything specific to add."

I remained silent but visible, so she could complete her rendering of me and, when I could tell she was finished, became a mist again and hovered over her shoulder to see how she saw me. She was a very talented artist; the picture she had drawn was as close to a photograph as a pencil could produce. Having not been concerned with my appearance now that I no longer had a body, I studied the picture with interest. The image I saw on paper was vaguely familiar; it had stared back at me from a mirror many times. Memories of running a razor over stubbly hair growing from my chin, combing back hair that had fallen over my forehead, adjusting a square cap on my head as I prepared to go somewhere. I saw myself giving my reflection a wink before turning to leave the room. This whole episode took less than a few seconds of my time and told me nothing about myself other than that I was a good-looking guy who took care of himself.

"If I have a picture of you, I might be able to circulate it online and see if anyone recognizes you." Her voice filled the void created by my musings.

"The what?" None of what she was saying made sense to me. Books and movie theaters made sense, online did not. "Newspaper?" I was not aware until later that what I said was not always so clear as it sounded when I said it to her. Sometimes I was loud, at times quiet, and sometimes only certain words were heard.

Leaning over the side of her bed, she pulled what looked like another long book from beneath it. She turned the book on its side, opening it upwards, revealing what looked like a small screen with images that changed as she pushed letters on a flat board beneath it. Apparently, I had been out of the world too long, there were lots of things I had missed. "I can post something on this thing that will travel around the world electronically and help me reach a lot of people in a short period of time." She pulled out a smaller flat device which she pointed at the drawing. In a second, the image from it appeared on the larger screen, and after typing a few words, she pushed a button and closed the lid of the object she had been working on.

"I work on this device all the time. Please don't short this thing out, not only is it going to help me find out something about you, it's also going to be my only source of income until I find another job." With a stern look on her face, she removed the towel from her head, fluffed her short hair and disappeared into the bathroom with an armful of clothes she had taken from a dresser near the bed. While she was getting dressed, I hovered close to the bathroom waiting for her. I had no desire to drift through the door and see her naked. At this point, she was more like a pet to me than a sex object. I already felt an ownership based on the connection we had made. While there was no deep love or other affection for her on my part, I had no intention of losing contact when I needed her so much.

It was while waiting for her in this manner that I made my first significant discovery about another thing I could do with my energy. Maddie had finished dressing sooner than expected and I, who had not bothered to move, felt her walk directly through me. Unlike my previous encounter with the dead old lady who made me feel as if I would choke on her presence, this was terrific! The feeling of her living flesh was wonderful and electric; blood coursed through her veins and the steady beating of her heart made me feel alive. She breathed, and I could feel the expansion of her chest as if I was breathing with her. The whole encounter took only a few seconds and, though I didn't want it to, ended abruptly. Her brain protested my presence and some kind of chemical reaction occurred, I could feel it rejecting me, pushing me out. Maddie moved, jerking herself away from my essence with a grimace. Shivering as if she had been standing in a deep freeze, she looked very tired and slightly sick to her stomach.

"What just happened?" Her tone was accusing and exhausted at the same time.

"I'm sorry," I said quietly. "I should have moved. It won't happen again." Yet even as I made her this assurance, I kept the encounter in the back of my mind, retreating to the corner of the room to become invisible again, waiting and watching her every move, conserving the energy I had absorbed from her so I could remain in her world.

Chapter Ten- Maddie

My first actual physical encounter with Perry was troubling, like participating in a marathon I hadn't trained for; it hurt and exhausted me. I walked out of the bathroom and straight into a cold mist that was whatever Perry had become; both strangely empty and filled with many things at the same time. Anger, frustration, sorrow, surged through my body but they were more like diluted echoes from the past than strong emotions. He was a memory that had invaded my reality; it felt weird and wrong. I didn't mind helping him, but this type of thing would never happen again. Even though the whole episode had lasted less than a few seconds, I was worn out. He had acted as though it was an accident, but I wasn't so sure. I was shaken, tired, and found myself sleeping again for several more, thankfully uneventful hours. When I woke, he was still in the room; he wasn't visible, but I could feel him quietly hanging around, watching me. I was just glad it was him for a change and not the dark thing that was conspicuously absent since his return. In fact, it suddenly occurred to me that *It* had not appeared to me at the same time as him since I encountered them. The only connection there seemed to be between the two was that they were aware of each other.

I was of two minds in this matter - relief at not having to deal with the scary thing and a little dread at having to deal with Perry. What if I wasn't up to the task of finding out who he had been and he didn't take it well? I remembered his decided lack of humor at my naming him and his eager desperation for me to solve the mystery of his past. When I stopped to think about it, it was overwhelming. I had my own baggage now; jobless except for the small income I made selling my art on-line to small businesses and a few loyal customers I had acquired over the years. I needed to come up with a plan to survive. I had filed an insurance claim against the cow's owner but, until that was settled, my meager earnings would hardly help me afford to live like an adult should. I had so much going on in my head, and now there was all this to add to it. It was exciting to delve into the unknown, but the unknown was scary and unpredictable, and I wasn't sure how to deal with it.

"What's wrong?" Perry's disembodied voice addressed me.

Suppressing a sigh and putting on my best game face, I stood up from the bed and straightened my rumpled clothing, "Nothing," I lied, determined to fake my way through the situation until I got really good at making it work. "How long have I been asleep?"

"Hours," the short and not very happy reply came to me. He was not showing himself and I was already aware that it meant he was reserving his energy to stay in my world. This realization comforted me because it meant he had weaknesses too, and added it to my knowledge of how to protect Maddie mental library. I excused myself one more time to put fresh, unwrinkled clothing on, fired up my laptop, checked my art for sale website, and settled a few money accounts. All the while he quietly hung in the background, radiating impatience, while I looked at the posting of his picture I'd circulated as a drawing made from a photograph of an unidentified man. Appealing to the adventurous crowd, I'd asked if there was anyone out there who could help me find who this man was. Though my posting had many views and comments, there was still no answer to my query. I looked once again at Herbert Delmont's site to make sure my name had not actually been broadcast, giving a silent sigh of relief when I saw nothing on his regularly updated posts.

"Find anything?" the weak voice whispered in my ear.

"Not yet, but people are looking." My remaining lamp flickered and dimmed as Perry drew energy from it.

"Please don't break it." I was aware of his effect on my stuff and couldn't afford to lose anything else.

He didn't speak again. I couldn't tell if it was because he was still mad at me or just running out of energy. Then I heard it, the faint ringing of my phone.

A quick look told me that it was my mother and, knowing she'd worry if I didn't answer, I pushed the accept button and made myself sound chipper.

"Hi, honey!" she said, obviously pleased with my alert and happy tone. "You sound good." I was glad at this point that she couldn't see me because I was sure I didn't look like I sounded. "What are you doing?"

"Well, I slept for a while and I'm going to finish some jobs on my site before posting my resume," I was saying all the right things while hoping I could get my crap together to make all this true.

"That's wonderful!" she said. I could picture her smiling and vowed to make sure I did what I'd claimed.

"I'm really busy today," Mom stated, pausing as if uncertain she, who had done so much to help me out since the accident, could possibly ask me to do something for her. "I mean, I could go to the store after I get off," she continued, "but since you're at home, I thought maybe you could go for me and get a few things for dinner."

My poor mother finished hurriedly, as if apologizing for having the nerve to ask a favor at all. I knew she was also thinking of the fact that I would have to drive a car for the first time since my accident.

"It's okay, Mom. I can do it," my cheerful voice filled the anxious silence, reassuring her I was up to the task. Dad was out of town on a business trip and I knew his car was still in the garage. "It will be good for me to get out of the house, I'd be glad to go shopping for you."

"Well, okay then, dear, I sure would appreciate it." I could hear the relief in her voice as she told me she loved me, to be safe, and hung up.

"I'm going out," I said to the air, as if he hadn't already heard the entire conversation I just had with my mother.

I was greeted with a disapproving silence, accompanied by a severe drop in room temperature that signaled Mr. Frosty's displeasure at my non-Perry related activity. I was getting pretty tired of that habit. "Well, fine," I said, and with a disgusted sneer I grabbed a jacket, went into the hall, and with Dad's car keys grasped tightly in my shaky hand, left the house.

Chapter Eleven-Perry

She left the house. I followed her; what other choice did I have? I was still in her world, there was no way I was going to lose sight of her; she was my anchor to all I used to be part of. I just had a feeling that it was better to know where she was, especially since I had seen the dark thing watching the entrance to her world. Out of all the people it could have sought out, it chose the same one I had. There had to be a reason for that. It seemed a strange coincidence that the darkness and I had picked the same person. Well, it wasn't going to get her. I hadn't seen it since we were together, maybe that meant it was gone. I'd stay close just to be sure. I'd gone through a lot to find her again; she'd better come up with some results soon. Other than typing some words on a screen, she hadn't done much to find out who I was, and I was going to watch her like a hawk until she did something to help me. I wasn't sure how long I'd been gone when I got lost but since returning to her side I had the sneaking suspicion she was hiding something from me. She was different in ways I couldn't quite put my finger on, giving me yet another reason to monitor her closely. I didn't make a sound as I passed through the metal of her car and hitched a ride. I knew she was aware of my presence but was too uptight to speak at the moment.

When I first found her, I'd learned that her death had been caused by a car accident. From her reaction to sitting behind the wheel, I was sure this was the first time she had driven since then. She was sweating, her breath erratic as she fought a panic attack. I was impressed with her fortitude as she swallowed her fear, inserted the key, and started the vehicle; maybe there was more to her than I first thought. Backing out of the garage was an ordeal too. She did so like an eighty-year-old lady with very poor vision. After what seemed like an eternity, we finally made it on to the road. Her hands gripped the steering wheel so tightly I could almost hear the plastic crack. She kept the car straight between the yellow lines on the left and the white lines on the right side of the road. Creeping along like a snail, she was tensing up, fear seeping into the air until I could practically see it swimming around her head in shades of brown and orange. These emotions were unpleasant and undignified, making her aura strangely exciting to me. Fear was something oh so familiar; not mine, other people's. This gave me yet another unpleasant insight to who I might have been. I had strong reactions to killing and fear and I didn't know why, but it didn't speak well of my character. It would have been so much better to be drawn to kittens and homeless people, with a strong urge to help both in some significant and saintly way, but none of those feelings had come out yet. There had to be an explanation for all this, I was sure I had been a good man.

After traveling a few miles, we were progressing toward a row of buildings that included clothing shops, a hardware store and a grocery store among others. Maddie eased into the parking lot and chose a space so far from the store it took her several minutes to hike through the long concrete expanse, passing several vehicles and a few people returning to their cars. Now that she was on solid ground, my earthly companion moved with more confidence. Her feet were steady as she grabbed a shopping cart. While she was engaged in this activity, I noticed the atmosphere around her became ugly. The source of the ugliness came from the direction of one of the stores. There was a muddy brown sludge-like aura approaching her. I saw it before I saw the person it was attached to. Unlike the dead, the living had readily identifiable auras hanging around their bodies. It told me right away whether they were good, bad, or open to entities like me. Maddie's energy was tuned to mine, uniquely identifiable among all others, but this energy was mean and angry.

I followed the sludge to a small woman in a blue jacket exiting the food market with a bag in her hand. The second she saw Maddie, her eyes bulged, lips drew downward, as she approached my person with a speed that belied her bent and frail frame. This person seemed to know Maddie, and from her body language, didn't like her at all. Driven by curiosity, I moved over to the woman, hovering close enough to see gray hairs poking out among the dark and red ones on top of her head. A strong odor of cigarette smoke clung to the old woman's skin; I heard wheezing as she quickened her steps to reach Maddie, who, oblivious to the impending encounter, had begun to push her shopping cart toward the store.

Like any interested by-stander, I was curious to see what happened next, but a nagging sense of guilt compelled me to call out a warning, "Maddie!" Her head snapped up just a split second before the old woman spoke out in a shrill voice. With an irritated glance in my direction,

Maddie passed on her displeasure at my not giving her time to avoid what was sure to be an ugly scene.

"Louise," she spoke through tight lips while continuing to push the cart toward the store.

"I guess the reports of your death weren't true." From the way Louise said it, I gathered she wasn't happy about that.

"That's right, I'm still alive." Maddie didn't slow her footsteps in her quest to reach the store, clearly hoping Louise would get the hint and go away.

"Yes, I can see you are." Louise stepped in front of the cart so that Maddie was forced to swerve to the side to avoid running into her. "Not only are you alive, you are also freely walking around."

Moving to her left, Maddie didn't say anything, seeking only to propel the cart to its destination. But the old woman would have none of it, she moved in the same direction, determined to speak. "Aren't you going to ask how Joe is doing?"

"No, I'm not," came the short reply.

"He's still in prison! And it's costing me a fortune in protection money just to make sure he doesn't get raped or stabbed!" Louise was shrieking now, spittle flew in the air, a few drops landing on the metal cart.

"Not my problem." Maddie pushed the cart to the right, intent on reaching the store without further contact with the unpleasant hag. But the old woman was surprisingly agile, counteracting the evasive move with another one of her own, blocking the way.

"Not your problem! You're his wife. The least you could do is give me some money to help him out! A visit or two would be nice. He hasn't seen you for a long time!"

"I was his wife, Louise. We haven't been married for years. Please go away."

I saw the shift in her posture before the purse came up and swung at Maddie's head. Without hesitation, I lunged forward, diverting her arm until it swung around and smacked her own back. Louise, caught completely off guard by my presence in her body, jerked around in an awkward semi-circle before stumbling over the shopping cart and onto the ground.

Moving her around was easy. In fact, gaining entry into her artery-clogged, black-lunged body had been incredibly simple. While swimming

51

around in the negative atmosphere that was Louise, it suddenly dawned on me that her weak character is what allowed me to enter in the first place. She, unlike Maddie, who was accessible to me because of her death, was not strong enough inside to resist, and that was a useful realization for me. It was great to be temporarily in control of something and I got a little carried away. Raising Louise from the ground with a rapidity that was amazing for a woman in such bad shape, I did an awkward little jig and smiled at Maddie.

"Wow! Her bladder is full." I could feel Louise protesting from somewhere deep inside her foggy little mind. But it didn't matter, I didn't have to leave if I didn't want to, and she couldn't make me. "You didn't tell me you were married," I said, using Louise's gruff vocal chords to speak.

"It never came up, I'm not anymore, and it's none of your business," she snapped, glaring at me, or my temporary puppet, as it were. "Would you please get out of her?" she said, keeping her voice low as to not attract any more attention. My dark-haired connection to this world looked nervously around, relaxing a little when she noticed there were only a few people moving toward the store and they weren't paying attention to her and Louise at all.

I stared at her through bleary eyes for a second more. "With pleasure." I was feeling pretty crappy from hanging around in this cesspool of a human being. So, taking whatever energy I could from Louise, I slipped out, feeling urine run down her leg as I left.

With a sigh of relief and nothing further to say, Maddie turned and walked away, leaving a confused and exhausted ex-mother-in-law standing alone in the parking lot. Tired and unsure of what just happened, but otherwise unharmed, Louise stared at her retreating back and didn't say another word to her as she entered the store.

Chapter Twelve-Maddie

My shopping experience started out awkwardly. As distracted as I had been after watching what Perry had done to Louise, I'd had to endure twenty minutes of his whispering excuses as to why he'd done it. I don't know why he bothered to say anything; I didn't believe a word of it. A small part of me had been happy he'd cut her tirade short. Experience told me it wouldn't have lasted much longer, but it would have ended in a scene the town would still be talking about months from now. I was awfully tired of that, hoping after all this time that she would have picked another target for her anger. The diversion was welcome, but I still wasn't enough of a jerk to see her harmed. This new skill Perry had exhibited was disturbing, making that frail old body do exactly what he wanted. I could tell she was partially aware that something was happening but her glazed eyes and confused look told me she wasn't quite sure what it was. I was also aware that she was now afraid of me. I guess that part was good. Mentally, I stopped myself from enjoying it too much. I didn't want to become a freak and Perry, well, he was getting more than a bit scary. I thought our chance encounter earlier in the day was uncomfortable and had almost believed it was an accident, now I wasn't so sure. I went through the motions of picking out vegetables, meat, cereal, and anything else I thought mother might need, while greeting old friends and acquaintances who were surprised I was already up and about.

Not everybody here hated me, only Joe's family. I was popular all through high school until my disastrous marriage. Everyone walked away from me after repeated warnings of marrying below my evolutionary level. After word of the divorce got out, everyone started talking to me again. I guess I was alright without jerk man. They were right, of course, so I didn't hold it against them. After forty-five minutes of roaming through the store, I began to enjoy being out again on what must have been shopping day for most of the people I knew. It was a great distraction because it allowed me to ignore the presence tagging along beside me and interact with normal, living people. Overall, it was a better afternoon than I had expected until I had to walk back to the car and drive home.

As soon as I loaded the groceries into the trunk and slid into the driver's seat, panic began to set in again. I took a minute to gather my nerves and turn the key, almost jumping through the roof when Perry broke the silence. "Took you long enough. When did food shopping become social hour?"

"Sometime after you died, apparently," I said. It slipped out before I thought about it. I tensed up waiting for an earful, but he just laughed; it was like a small breeze going past the side of my face.

"Look, I can still carry on my life while helping you," I said. He appeared in the passenger seat, looking a little more solid than earlier, no doubt highly energized by his contact with Louise and the shorting out of several electrical systems in the store. He didn't speak, just sat there staring at the scenery we passed on the way back to my parents' house. I was much more relaxed on the return trip, going only slightly under the speed limit, less afraid of death than I was on the way to the store. What was it they said about riding a bike? You never forget, but you do stop faster and jump at any sign of an approaching car. "You're doing better," he said, sharing that supportive observation.

"Thanks," I replied, as he looked silently out at the highway we were traveling on. Fence posts strung with wire continued for miles, the only other objects visible were a few large billboards advertising stores in the shopping center we had just left. Brightly colored images and lettering proudly announced the best shopping experience ever, with arrows pointing to a turnoff that would take drivers back to our previous location. A few miles from the house now, I was feeling much better about handling the car than when I had started out. Relaxing into the comfortable leather seat like my old driving self. I was closing in on the small road leading to my childhood home when Perry did something that scared the crap out of me, canceling out the calm confidence I had acquired on this leg of my journey. "Stop; stop; stop!!" he shouted. I skidded to an abrupt stop on the gravel covered shoulder.

Trying to steady my shaking hands and slow my heart rate, I paused before turning to look at my shady companion who had already exited the vehicle through the door. You know, really *through* the closed door, and was now hovering in mid-air in front of a billboard I had passed twenty-feet ago. Opening my own door, getting out the old-fashioned way, I stomped along the gravel covered shoulder to the large sign behind me. Moving around to the front of the large advertisement he was studying so intently, I swallowed anger, fear, and the urge to scream at him. The picture on it was old. I had seen it many times in the years before

I moved out; it was old even then. Most of the formerly bright colored paper, faded after exposure to the elements, had been stripped off, revealing several layers of old ads, the most prominent a picture of a camel smoking a cigarette. Perry was looking at it with interest.

"I think I used to smoke." The muted tone of his voice didn't convince me this had been worth my minor nervous breakdown, and I was about to tell him that when I saw something that made the hairs on the back of my neck rise to full attention. Still visible to the side of the camel's head were the bold words: IS IT ALWAYS ILLEGAL TO KILL A WOMAN? and a thin strip of yellow with hints of other colors underneath clinging to the wooden surface around it. I got the impression that it was more the focus of his intense stare than the stupid smoking camel. I waited for clarification that didn't come before speaking.

"Well, that's just great!" I tried to put the anger back in my voice so he would think I hadn't noticed the other thing. "Do you think maybe you could let me know some other way than almost giving me a heart attack?" He turned to look at me for a second, eyes a flat black color, devoid of emotion causing a chill down my spine. I stared back, not wanting to show my fear, not wanting him to know what I was thinking. It seemed an eternity before, giving me a sheepish grin, he dissolved into a gray mist, the words "I'm sorry," whispered in my ear.

Without glancing backward, I slowly walked to the car and started it up to drive back home, all the while aware Perry was there with me, watching every move I made.

Chapter Thirteen-Perry

He called today and talked to her for an hour. Her cheeks got red and she had this goofy look on her face. That Damen was taking up my time. She was supposed to be helping me. And days after we had no response to her enquiry, she was just doing her own thing. Living her life, selling artwork on the *computer* as she called it, and receiving sums of money on that same machine. Other time was occupied with calls from an insurance man, and her parents who were home most nights. I wasn't allowed to talk to her while they were around. It was all beginning to drain me. It required a lot of power to stay in this world; the effort of it made me feel thin and stretched out. I had to move away to find more energy. It was then that I found I could leave her for a little while, moving short distances to observe things and seek out more power, finding it just down the road from street lights and sometimes neighboring houses. I found myself often going back to that billboard, trying to find a reason it had caught my attention. It wasn't necessarily the ad about killing a woman that I was familiar with, it was the message. Why did it always come back to death with me?

I had seen her looking up that advertisement on her machine. It was a harmless ad about postage stamps; it meant nothing to me. The fact that she looked it up, told me she noticed it too. Its significance didn't register with her either. Other than her usual annoyance with me, I hadn't sensed any hesitation on her part to help. In fact, I think she was growing to like me a bit more. True, we hadn't made much progress in our search for my identity, but I hadn't given her much to work with. How is it that I could see so much in this world, high above it all like an all-seeing eye, but couldn't affect much? Other than a few teasing glimpses of useless information, I had nothing to contribute about myself. I was here again and had just finished shorting out the street light a few feet from the billboard when I felt the need to check on Maddie. It was just past breakfast time; her parents would be at work, making this the perfect time for me to talk to her. My essence vibrated, renewed by the intake of power. I was about to return to my person when I noticed the truck coming down the road. Red paint peeled off the hood and side panels; it looked nothing like the generic automobiles I'd seen in the parking lot and traveling up and down these very roads. No, this vehicle looked more like something I would have driven. This realization thrilled me. The truck had a dome roof with a long hood, short bed in the back, and prominent wheel covers; just like one I remembered getting into many a morning. Except the truck I remembered was new with a shiny coat of blue paint. I wondered what year this model was.

Intrigued by this wondrous event, I moved through the door panel to hover unseen above several bulky bags on the passenger seat. I had seen the driver before on his usual mail delivery route, but this wasn't the vehicle he had used. Small and thin, the man was dressed neatly with a ball cap perched on top of his head. Calm, and unaware I was there, humming softly to a song on the radio, the middle-aged gentleman radiated a pleasant, welcoming aura. I stared at him in wonder as he continued to drive slowly from mailbox to mailbox, reaching through me to an open bag filled with envelopes separated into stacks and secured with rubber bands. Each stack had a small sticker with an address on the top which the man read before sliding them into the box. I stayed with him for a couple of miles, studying him and thinking. This man was unguarded, an open container with no negative energy hanging around. It occurred to me that, while he wasn't weak like that old drunk woman whose body I had walked in, he was just as useable. The idea that I could live again, even for a short while in another body was exciting. I had done it once and I could do it again. His aura told me that he wasn't gifted, that he saw only the solid physical world around him, and didn't know there was anything he had to protect himself from. For me, he was perfect. As he came to a stop at the next mailbox, I moved through him and made myself at home. Hands gripping the steering wheel tightly to still their shaking, I stared at my new gaunt face and smiled. With the faint echo of the man's protest ringing far back in his head, I set the car in gear and drove toward Maddie's house.

Chapter Fourteen-Maddie

Damen left a few hours ago. He drove over just after Perry left, showing up on my doorstep like a perfectly timed surprise. It felt so good not to have my ghostly chaperone here that I took advantage of the time we had alone and enjoyed his company. I had promised myself I wasn't going to see him anymore but when he kept calling, I just couldn't help myself. He was funny and charming and openly admitted he was crazy about me. I was becoming quite attached but still couldn't confide in him about Perry. So I lived this double life, talking to a dead man, and flirting with a wonderful living man. I was trying to get my life back together, all the while aware that I still had to solve this puzzle for Perry. I hadn't told him yet but I'd met an enthusiastic criminology student named Dave on-line. He was helping do research on my missing person case. Though he hadn't found anything yet, I was hopeful he could help me finish this so Perry and I could move on to our respective destinies. Despite my misgivings, I had begun to like Perry. Ghost guy could be quite charming when he wanted, offering little memories that were, at best, only generic and not specific to when or where he might have lived. But it was nice that he was contributing. The longer my dead friend lingered, the less desperately he clung to me; moving away occasionally to explore his surroundings and, no doubt, to suck up the energy he needed to stay in this world. While he was away, I had been doing a little extra research on supernatural encounters and abilities. I wasn't quite sure how reliable it was since none of my experts had died and come back to life, but I did learn more about keeping bad things out of my head. I vowed to stay as active and positive as I could, keeping a strong self-image to prevent any negativity from working its way into my life. It was working. I had been sleeping better, without any interference from Perry. I had also had two more episodes of that out of body thing I'd experienced before. They seemed to happen when I was very tired and still scared me a lot. My trips were short and only around the room. I was always grateful to be back in my body, especially since I wasn't sure how I'd gotten out of it in the first place, but thankfully this had stopped. Overall, things were getting better even though I was feeling my specter's increasing frustration at my lack of results.

Yes, things had been improving and this had been an especially lovely day. I savored it, deserved it. It helped me to forget, for a while, about the visions. They had become a part of my life I was trying to manage along with my budding romance, tenuous employment status, and role as spiritual investigator for a dead man. The darkness had stopped trying to visit my dreams, undoubtedly because Perry was with me but, since his behavior had adapted to my schedule, so had *It's*.

The darkness had come when I was alone, and thankfully, still in my body, sending the strongest emotions into the air, emotions I was sensitive enough to notice. It showed me there was more than one way to get through and it wasn't going to give up. Panic, pain, and shock transmitted themselves to me, sharing some kind of unexpected and unpleasant surprise until I forced it out of my head. These daily unexplained and unwanted visits accompanied by intense fear were getting harder and harder to fight. I could make it go away but it always returned and was able to subject me to a few minutes of shared terror each time. But as quickly as they started, they stopped and I, foolishly optimistic soul that I was, thought I was down to just one dead visitor at a time. I got comfortable with the time of silence and relief, believing that I was so strong, impressive, and oh so mentally powerful.

The past weeks had been great, today was great. Maybe it really would be okay. In a final salute to the Maddie-had-it-all-under-control illusion, the darkness decided to screw up what was left of this perfect day and pay me a visit shortly after Damen left. Two minutes of smiling and recalling his intoxicating kisses, and I turned to find it swimming around in my living room. This, of course, meant it had been watching me and had not gone back into the dead place as I thought. I should have known that it, like Perry, had an agenda that included me. Why else would it stalk me? I was suddenly the center of unwanted attention and I didn't know why.

It had returned with a determination that was terrifying. The feelings it sent were so intense I almost lost my composure, forgetting everything I had learned about protecting myself. Breathing just a little bit too fast and gripping the back of Dad's recliner with frozen fingers, I almost gave in to the panic that would make me an open target for that thing. Here it was again, radiating a need so urgent I could taste it. With a resigned sigh, I considered my options. Maybe if I let it have its say, we could be done with this and it could move on. I guess it sensed my unspoken consent and reached out a thin shaky extension of itself, touching my head. Out of some instinct I would have normally resisted with every fiber of my being, I allowed it to make contact. I don't know why. It was a stupid impulse. As if I could begin to understand any of my choices since returning from death; like helping Perry, for instance. I really didn't have any guidelines to follow and no one to ask about the soundness of my decisions. I did what I normally did, I faced it on my own, like an idiot.

At first, there was a stabbing pain in the center of my chest, followed by disbelief and the knowledge that I was dying. Well, not me, exactly. I was picking up the entity's thoughts and feelings. It was a short but very powerful encounter, passing on the last minutes of whatever, or whomever, the darkness had been. I'm guessing a murder victim by the unexpected nature of its passing, it seemed surprised at being taken from the world so quickly. I'm sure I would have learned more, had I allowed it. After a few minutes of this horrid shared experience, it departed. I fell to the ground fighting the strong urge to vomit up the contents of the lovely lunch Damen and I had eaten. I'm not sure how long I sat there trying to figure out what all this meant, trying not to remember the events as if they were not my own but someone else's; fear, pain, and the knowledge I was being forced form this world against my will. It wasn't me, I'm alive. That's what gave me the strength to recover, stand on my feet and get my act back together. Of course, it took a good twenty minutes to come that far. Pacing back and forth, breathing deep and concentrating on my surroundings helped a lot. Looking at the table to my left, chairs by the window, all the ordinary things that indicated I was safe in my parent's house. I was just about as back to normal as I was going to get, when I heard the mailman pull up outside. Straightening up to full height, I tried to look a little more dignified, less scared, and concentrated on interacting with a living person. Jeff, our mailman was about an hour late. I found that a bit odd since he was normally on time. I also noticed he was driving that truck he'd been restoring. He had been working on it for years and talked about it a lot, but I hadn't seen him take it out for a spin in almost a year. He must be almost finished with it, I thought. This being a rather small town, people liked to stop and talk during their daily routine. Jeff often extended his mail drop for a minute or two to chat and I'd often see him around town, so I felt I knew him rather well. This kind man had lived here all his life, most of it alone, his wife having passed away when I was in grade school. While there were rumors of an active love life with a few single women in town, he'd never married again. Always pleasant, I'd never heard an unkind word spoken about him. I liked him very much and had talked to him more often since I'd returned from the hospital. He'd approached me when I'd returned home and seemed so concerned about me, asking all kinds of questions about my life. It was a little confusing to be the object of interest like that, but he'd explained that my near miss, had made him regret not knowing me better, in a friendly way, he was quick to add. Walking to the door, I opened it to say hello and was greeted by a version of Jeff that scared the hell out of me.

Chapter Fifteen-Perry

Driving this truck definitely brought back memories. Sitting on the soft springy seat, I admired the cab's interior. Though the outside was unpainted, the inside was pristinely restored with a shiny new dashboard, freshly carpeted floor, and slick red and white upholstery on the bench beneath my borrowed butt. Running *our* hand over the shiny material, I had a flashback of driving very slowly down a bumpy dirt road, eyes seeking just the perfect spot, some place I would remember and return to later. The thought of it made my skin tingle and mouth go dry with barely contained excitement. Why would that be? What could I possibly be looking for out in the country? Was I a hunter? Maybe that was it. I had to be. What else do people do in the woods? Accepting this explanation as the only logical one, and receiving no further insight into the past, I allowed myself the luxury of enjoying my loaner body. Gripping the wheel excitedly, I listened to the engine, so finally tuned it purred in my ears, and steered the truck down the sunlit road. I was so caught up in the secondhand impression of being alive, I passed Maddie's house entirely. I was miles down the road, driving at a good pace and enjoying the hell out of the day, before realizing. I was having such a great time controlling the vehicle, feeling the sunlight heat my cheek through the open window, the breeze ruffling my hair; it was the closest to paradise I could have desired. Turning the volume on the radio louder and humming along to a song I didn't recognize, I piloted my wondrous craft down the small road with faint confused rumblings of my host sounding in the background. Ignoring him, I drove a few minutes more before turning the truck onto a dirt road, pulling the gear shift downward to the white R. Backing out again, I narrowly missing a small car moving quickly down the road. The driver beeped and stuck her middle finger up, while I stomped on the break and jerked to a stop, smacking my head on the driver's window. It hadn't occurred to the driver to check and see if I was alright; the woman simply continued on her way as if this whole incident were just an unpleasant delay in her wild flight to wherever she was bound. Turning *our* bruised head to stare at the vehicle speeding away, I managed to get a look at the license plate and bright blonde hair of its driver. NOBRAKIN was emblazoned in blue letters on the flat tag of the little sport car. This must be a new thing, badly spelled words used to identify a car's owner; things used to be done differently. Outwardly calm, but silently seething, I kept the unique, but easy to remember information in mind for later use. Wiping the blood from *our* forehead, I wondered how this seemed an almost routine thing for me, taking note of details such as this. Maybe I had been a policeman of some kind. That would be a good thing to find out about myself. I'd have to keep that possibility in mind when I talked to Maddie again. Other than the bump on *our* head, we were unharmed, but I was disturbed and annoyed by what happened. Vowing to do a little research on the blue car, I looked back for more traffic before sliding the car in gear and toward Maddie's home.

I drove on, putting the unpleasant incident behind me, getting lost again in the sensation of living. The day was beautiful indeed and having a body to move about in was intoxicating. Fingers flexing and toes tapping, I performed the actions of an animated being once again. I guessed I was about a mile away from Maddie's house when I saw something I recognized. It was almost too good to be true. Sitting on the side of the road like a gift-wrapped present, sat a bright blue two-seater with the blonde driver who had so rudely whizzed by earlier. She was leaning against the car, right front tire now flat, waiting for a knight in shining armor to come along and save her. Well, this day just kept getting better and better. Visiting Maddie would just have to wait a little longer. This was a situation that needed my expertise. On seeing me, and apparently not recognizing the person she had just so rudely addressed, the woman leaned toward the road and waved her hand to attract my attention. With a smile as wide and friendly as had ever been seen, I pulled ahead of her car, wheels crunching on the gravel before sliding to a stop. Yes, this was indeed a wonderful day, I thought again as she came to my window and we began to speak. What a great day to have a body.

Chapter Sixteen-Maddie

Jeff was pale. His shirt was covered in thick red stuff that looked kind of like clay. I'd had the same stuff stuck to my shoes and shorts often enough when I'd played in the woods by the streams. Clay was a stubborn sticky material when wet and had to be scrubbed thoroughly to remove, as my mother often complained when she tried in vain to salvage my wardrobe. What in the world was Jeff doing covered in it as if he'd been tromping around in the woods in the middle of his appointed rounds? Not only was he a mess, but he looked scared, his eyes wide as saucers, as if communicating something different than his lips were about to say. But it wasn't until he smiled at me that chills went down my spine. His lips creased in a wide grin totally at odds with his panicked look. Jeff stepped into the house without being asked, and began to speak to me in an excited voice. "Did you see that truck! I used to drive one just like it." Perry knew he didn't have to identify himself. I already had the sick feeling he was present before he began to speak.

"Why did you take over Jeff?"

"It was the truck," he began again, as if this explanation was good enough to justify taking over the man's body.

"You have to leave him now!"

Jeff's spirit was screaming somewhere deep in his head. I could hear it in a way that I wouldn't have been able to had I not been working on improving my gift, or curse, whatever you'd like to call it. I could sense him in the way I could sense Perry, though maybe not as strongly.

"It was the truck," he repeated, and I knew I wouldn't be able to reason with him until he said what he had to say. "I recognized the truck and just had to drive it!" Jeff's voice was breathless as he tried to make me understand. "That truck was brand-new when I drove one! That's the time I'm from, I know it!"

I watched the excited expression on Jeff's face while his eyes continued to show that same panicked, pleading look. "That's great," I said, although my tone hardly conveyed this statement. I just wanted him to get out of Jeff. "What did you do to him?" I pointed to Jeff's muddied shirt and messy clothes.

"We just changed a tire." Perry shook his head and smiled. "It's been awhile since I've done that. It's a good thing that tires haven't changed much."

Looking at my companion within my friend, I wasn't quite sure if I was getting the whole story but was sure that pressing him for more would only force him to lie and prolong his presence in Jeff's body. Nodding to appease him, I was more worried about getting him to vacate the mailman.

"What year is that truck?" The conversation continued as if he had no idea he was causing his shell any discomfort. I knew he was aware of this, and I was pretty sure it didn't bother him one bit.

"Oh, come on!" His tone was cheerfully disbelieving. "I'm not hurting him. At most, he'll be really tired." Of course, he knew how I felt. I'm sure, as hard as I was trying not to show what I was thinking, my face was betraying me.

"Find out what year that truck is, and I'll leave his body." He spoke as if this were a reasonable thing he had every right to ask. This made me angry, I had to swallow my original comment and make my statement neutral. There would be no argument while he was in that body.

"Why don't you just ask Jeff? After all he's the one who's been working on it."

A moment of silence and a sheepish look from my companion. "I can't really maintain control and let him think and talk on his own." A shiver went down my spine when he said this with little regret; his cold tone while discussing this man as a puppet made me again wonder exactly who I was dealing with.

"If you really intend to let him go, then let him talk. What he tells me can help me narrow down my search."

Our eyes met. I was struck by the flat stare I couldn't read. There was no sign of Jeff in there, just someone determined to stay put while I was asking him to leave. This all lasted a few agonizing seconds until thankfully, Perry had second thoughts, as I was facing a very confused Jeff who was really Jeff again.

"Maddie?"

"Hi, Jeff, nice to see you again," I said as if we were beginning a normal conversation while trying not to show him how guilty I was feeling about what had happened to him. "What happened to your shirt?" With each word, I sunk lower and lower in my own eyes.

Hesitation followed by a glance downward to his muddied clothing. "I think I may have changed a tire." It was more of a question than a firm statement. I could tell it took a lot of self-control for him not to break down in front of me. Nodding awkwardly, the mailman stood for a moment, unsure of what to do or say. I scrambled to fill in the blanks for him, to normalize the day so he wouldn't be permanently traumatized by this event.

"Wow, it's really hot out there today! You must have overdone it," I said. "I'll bet you were working on that truck until you came to work today and then driving all along your route without a break. Did you forget to eat lunch again?"

Squinting his eyes, as if trying to remember and make that part of his reality, Jeff nodded and allowed himself to be escorted to the kitchen, where I, barely a cook, managed to whip up a grilled cheese sandwich and some chips I found in the cabinet.

It's all just normal, see? Rattling on, as if this were like every other conversation we'd ever had, I managed to relax my dazed companion and get him to focus on how ordinary the day was.

"I see the truck is almost finished. When are you going to have it painted?"

"Next week." Beginning to warm up to the reality I was giving him, the conversation now centered on his passionate hobby.

"What color?"

He paused for a moment and looked puzzled, "I was going to say blue, but I know it should be red to match the interior." Whatever input he'd picked up from Perry was fading and Jeff was taking control again. All that had occurred before rapidly faded into a bad day of heat-exhaustion.

"That should look sharp," I said.

He looked tired, I needed to ask the question soon. Perry hung in the air radiating impatience at what he perceived as a delay, and I didn't want him bothering Jeff again. "What year did you say it was again?"

"Oh, it's a 1936 Ford Model T with an inline four-cylinder engine." A tired smile lit up his face. "Parts are very hard to come by, that's why it took so long to finish."

We talked a bit longer, Jeff and I, before he admitted he was tired and wanted to go home. I was the last stop on his route, no one would be expecting him to be on time for anything. After all he'd been through, I wanted to offer him a place to take a nap but was afraid to have him so vulnerable with Perry around. After receiving thanks for my hospitality, I watched him go, knowing I had done him no particular favor. I considered Perry's presence here my fault, and his actions, by default, my responsibility. I couldn't admit that to the poor man and not have him run away in fear. Pretending all was good, I looked on as he drove toward town.

"Have I really been gone that long?" the disembodied voice whispered in my ear. I heard sadness, disbelief, and a bit of anger too. I would have felt badly for him had I not seen what he just did to a living person to obtain this information.

"Let's find out. We can use that date as a reference, but for all we know you could have restored it just like Jeff did." Though I didn't say anything, Perry knew I was angry. I'm sure at this point my face was screaming disapproval.

"I'm really sorry I had to do that," he said.

Once again, I was struck by the almost monotone apology. I knew he wasn't sorry but wasn't sure if that's because he was desperate to discover who he was or because he needed to say this to keep me pacified. I felt him leave the room just as my dad pulled into the drive, uttering a few parting words as he disappeared.

"Find out who I was."

Chapter Seventeen-Perry

Being in that body was both energizing and exciting. I had left it with great reluctance because I knew Maddie wanted me to. Letting her find out what I wanted was more important than my entertainment. I had been inside the man, wearing him like a suit, but would not let him have enough control to push me out. Any active, independent thought on his part would have been bad for me. I worked with the element of surprise, rushing into the unsuspecting host, carrying with me all that I was, for as long as I occupied the space. While in that person, there was no room for what they were, it had to be suppressed for me to stay awhile. The feelings I'd experienced were still so fresh. It was like being drunk on the best wine I'd ever consumed, I didn't want it to end. I replayed the memories again and again. I had enjoyed my temporary occupation. The little man was older than I would have liked to wear, but he was still quite charming and useful. I didn't think he was much to look at, but it seemed he was well-known and made those he met comfortable. Take that cheesy little blonde woman we met with the attention span of a hyperactive toddler, who, having no memory of flipping me off, was all kindness and light when *we* fixed her tire. She knew who he was, had heard of his prowess with women, a fact I found both interesting and hard to believe. Blondie was more than willing to set up a rendezvous with the little guy, reminding him more than once exactly where she lived. I kept careful note of this address for future use, perhaps she would receive a visit. It might be fun. All kinds of possibilities ran through my head. I almost smiled, aching for things I might once again experience. Strong urges to make contact with a living being once again made me remember a few things, such as fond memories of driving that truck. I had been so proud of it, and that spacious bed in the back had come in handy for all kinds of things. I had brief flashbacks of sitting behind the wheel once again, sweat running down my face, chest tight, mouth dry. I had to go fast, had to be quick and quiet. Why? All the enjoyment I had been anticipating was gone with this new puzzle, a reminder of all the unanswered questions I carried with me. For a split second, fear of what I might have been made me hesitate. What was I? The sensations of secrecy and avoidance made me wonder again if maybe I had been a policeman of some kind, maybe a detective. Surely, I had been brave and clever. I felt I had avoided detection of some kind and couldn't see myself in any role but the good guy. I had to know more, there had to be more. I had slipped out of the mailman like a good little boy and hung around Maddie, listening to the conversation, and trying to think of what I knew about the year 1936. As they continued to babble on about things I no longer cared about, my mind tried to touch on something specific about that time-frame. That's when it happened again, that flash of a memory about walking in the hallway of a school. Concentrating really hard, I slowed the vision down and paid particular attention to the smiling people greeting me as I made my way to the locker. Boys wore cloth pants, neatly pressed; I didn't see many of those "jeans" Maddie had explained people were wearing now. The girls I saw were much more conservatively dressed than that woman I'd come across today, in longer skirts, higher necklines. All except for one girl. She had blonde hair and was wearing the tightest skirt and sweater I'd ever seen. Looking at her, I felt my heart race. I swallowed hard, clenching my fingers tightly at my side, trying to avoid adjusting the evidence of my approval. She was bad, and she knew it. Her eyes traveled downward, bright red lips smiled knowingly at me as she passed. I hated her at that moment; the way she made me feel so dirty, seeing a weakness no one else had. Rage, shame, and intense hunger gnawed at my insides as I continued to move through the wide corridor toward the locker I always reached at the end of the vision. I opened the metal door. With shaky hands, I reached for the books in front of me. But this time it went further. I closed the door and the dark-haired girl I'd seen before was standing there, smiling at me like she had so many times. Her smile calmed me. I was lost in a feeling of total love. She was clean and pure, nothing like that other one, but I couldn't remember her name. And then, just as quickly as it had begun, it was over, there was nothing more to see. Pondering this latest clue into my past, I watched my human puppet leave and spoke a few words to Maddie about the urgency of finding out more, never once mentioning what I'd seen. Apologizing, like I was supposed to, I tried to convince my human contact that I hadn't meant to take her friend but we both knew that wasn't true. I was more than happy to do it. After a minute or two of insincere exchanges, she seemed to relax. She wanted to believe me and give me the benefit of the doubt. I didn't make myself visible, afraid of showing my face to her, afraid of what my memories may reveal. I still needed her help, what her modern technology could find out for me. If I had to figure things out on my own I could be hanging out in limbo forever. Something was building in me; I'd been dormant too long. I needed answers. There were things I hadn't finished, and occupying flesh, even for a short time, brought back long sleeping desires. I was restless with a lot of energy, most of it drained from Jeff's body, a little bit from houses down the road. Snapping and crackling with all this power, I bid her goodbye after reminding her what she needed to do. Her father was returning, and I couldn't seem to stop thinking about the cheap blonde I'd seen in my vision, that woman on the side of the road was just like her. My encounter with Jeannie's spirit had been the same; memories of it brought a hunger so strong I had to move away from Maddie and into the fading light of approaching evening. Thoughts of an address came to me as I sped through the sky, I had a date to keep.

Chapter Eighteen-Maddie

I talked with Dad awhile longer knowing we were alone. It seemed Perry had gone off again. I found it interesting he wasn't spending every minute with me. Maybe he was beginning to adjust to our arrangement, trusting me to find out what he wanted. Maybe he really was ashamed of what he did to Jeff this afternoon. It had to be tempting to live again in someone's body, even for just a short time if you knew you could. I might have done the same had I been in his position. It looked like he had died relatively young. I know it had been quite a relief to find myself alive again after my close encounter with the afterworld; maybe if I'd had to stay longer, my perspective of the gray place would've been a little less uncertain. I guess the urge hits you after you've had a chance to think about it. If Perry was really from the 1930's, he'd had a lot longer to think about what he'd lost. I went with what I'd discovered, sending a message to Dave about the timeline of his search, having to do a little creative writing to come up with a reason I'd narrowed it down so precisely to that point in time. I told him I'd seen a photo in a bar, the man had been standing next to a truck. No one knew who he was other than his having been killed and I wasn't allowed to remove it. I sent him a sketch of said man and truck as if it came from a photo. I simply said that I wanted to use the image I had seen on the walls, and didn't want to get sued if the man had family who might object. Knowing it sounded farfetched, I kept it simple. After all, simple was easy to remember,

less embellishment was needed if I had to repeat it again. It was fortunate that he found this amusing, an exercise to develop his skills. Vowing to get back to me after he'd done some research, Dave logged off and I was left with nothing to do. Dad hadn't stayed long, just coming in to change before going to pick Mom up for dinner. He'd asked me if I wanted to go, but knowing this was date night for them, had been for many years, I declined. There is only one thing worse than being the third wheel on a night out on the town, and that's being one on your parents' dates. I could have had a date, I guess, but Damen was working. That was the only thing that kept me from feeling too sorry for myself. Though I was still having trouble considering him an actual steady boyfriend, we had gotten quite close. I hadn't slept with him yet; it was too awkward, considering I knew we were never really alone. Putting on that type of show for Perry wasn't really my style. I guess that made us just friends and not committed; mainly because if I told him what was really going on he might think I should be committed.

I sent Dad off, trying not to show any anxiety about being alone again. Not only was I alone, but it was unusually quiet. I sat up for hours, not sure whether I could relax because the darkness hadn't shown up the instant it had an opening. Remembering our last encounter was stressful. I didn't relish sharing the emotions of a terrified murder victim again. I wasn't even sure if it was the same darkness that had been following me since I came back. There might be more than one entity like it, all drawn toward my energy. Lucky me. Sitting on the couch, too wound up to do anything except wait, my butt began to fall sleep. I could hear the ticking of the grandfather clock in the front hall, marking the seconds, minutes, hours in which nothing happened.

I just couldn't seem to relax. This night was too damn ordinary, and I was no longer used to ordinary. I wasn't used to being alone for this long either; it was kind of creepy, which was hilarious because I'd seen, talked to, and been attacked by some very scary things. So now boring was the new source of terror. Rambling again, I couldn't stand it. Where was it, damn it! Eerie, uninterrupted silence drew out for the longest two minutes I'd ever experienced. I checked my watch once again. It usually waited for me to be alone and swooped down like a vulture trying to get its two cents in, making me steel myself against total control. I had shown I was ready for it and not willing to let it dominate me but that didn't mean I didn't have to fight it every time. Maybe I'd already scared it off with my impressive powers. I'd shown it I would be willing to help, but only on my terms, the same deal I'd made with Perry. I mean, he hadn't complained or thrown things around again, following the rules I'd set for my time. Tapping my feet nervously on the floor for what seemed an eternity, it finally occurred to me that since nothing was happening I could be getting some work done. My laptop was in the bedroom. I made my way to get it. Stretching my stress-stiffened muscles, I shook off my unease and walked a few steps into the dark cloud I hadn't even sensed arrive. Air so cold it raised every hair on my arm, surrounded me. Wild laughter reverberated in my head as the darkness gloried in the fact it had caught me off-guard. Showing me that I was very much mistaken about my overestimated strength, it had ambushed me. My arms flailed wildly at the thing that was nowhere but everywhere at the same time. I tried to get it off and out of me. But I was too late to stop the inevitable, it had already invaded my consciousness, taking me over, dragging me into whatever personal hell it had last experienced.

Branches crunched beneath my feet. I was standing in total darkness, afraid to move but afraid to stay still for too long. Looking back, I saw part of the vehicle I had just left parked about a hundred yards behind me. I had hurt him and escaped. Why in the hell was I still so close to it? I should have made it further away by now. He could be here any minute; where was he? The rough bark of the tree I was hiding behind scratched my hands as I peered anxiously around it, listening for any indication he was back on his feet. My whole body hurt. The arm I studied was pale and covered in deep scratches. Touching a scalp that wasn't mine, I discovered a gash at the hairline. It was sticky and made me dizzy. Breath coming out in harsh gasps created both by panic and the realization that it was so cold out here. Bare feet standing in deep snow, they were going numb as I waited for a sign that it was safe to move. Maybe I could take the car and just drive off, but I didn't know where he was, and I couldn't take the chance that he would find me. I was free for the moment but didn't know how long that would last. Hoping that the feeling of despair that had immobilized me was just temporary, and the reality of my impending death all wrong, I waited for an opening, a way out of the nightmare I was caught in. This was not how my evening had started. Why was this happening? This wasn't real, couldn't be real. I should be going home now; they were expecting me at work tomorrow. I had family who loved me and would wonder why I wasn't home. My life couldn't end this way! To delay the panic quickly overtaking me, I glanced furtively over my shoulder for any sign of civilization, a house or road I could make my way to and get some help. Maybe I could make it out of this. Maybe there was a chance I could survive and get home; I wanted to live so badly. I didn't deserve to die like this, I was a good person. Clamping my lips together to still my chattering teeth and hide the frosty puffs of air escaping them, I took a few careful steps back, sinking a few inches into the snow as I did. The car wouldn't help me. He would know if I went back there. I had to get further away and disappear into the woods behind me. I could hide some place and wait until he got tired of looking for me. Taking my chances with the elements was the least of my worries, after all people had survived the cold before; I'd read about it. Step by agonizing step, I kept to the tree line, slinking close to the ground when I had to cross open areas. Breathing a little easier when my last glance revealed I had left the car far behind me, I allowed myself to slow down a little while looking for a way to proceed further. That's when I saw it, a faint light to my left. Clinging to the tree I had hidden behind, I peered cautiously around it again to see light and a puff of smoke rising into the air, as if from the chimney of a house. It took several more minutes of careful study to realize that what I was seeing was real. The light stayed in place, smoke continued to stream upwards against the pale moonlight visible in the sky. Barely containing my excitement, I took a few steps toward the building which must have been a quarter of a mile away. Hope for a life beyond this made me almost crack a smile; I was wrong about the outcome, I had outsmarted him and was going to live after all. A step or two more through the pile of snow took me closer and closer to safety. I hoped whoever lived there had a gun. Surely anyone who lived this far out of town had a gun for protection. I would need them to be brave and prepared because I was going to live. They were going to help me stay alive. I was so close now, maybe a half hour more to get through the stinking snow that was slowing me up so much. I reached up to touch my head once again and found blood trickling down my face. Though I couldn't see it clearly, I knew it was blood, that sharp metallic odor drifted from my fingertips to my nostrils. I wiped my hand on my skirt and fought the dizziness that had begun to blur my vision. I guess I was hurt a little worse than I thought, but was still alive and I was going to make it to that house. Another step and my feet gave out on me. A muffled cry escaped my lips as I fell forward into the crunchy wet snow that was making my escape so difficult. No! I was so close! I had to make it! Raising up on feet I could no longer feel, feet that didn't seem to want to follow the instructions I was giving them, I looked longingly at the house whose outline had become clearer for just a second before a hand clamped over my mouth and strong arm dragged me backwards into the woods I had come from. Damn you! were the last words on my mind as I found myself sitting on my living room floor again, crying uncontrollably, the phone ringing loudly in the kitchen behind me.

Chapter Nineteen-Perry

I felt so good, better than I had felt since I'd been back. Flexing my new, strong hands and thick biceps, I decided this body was a much better fit than the little Casanova I'd worn earlier. I walked casually down the street, pulling the soft material of the thin jacket away from my impressive six-pack. Smiling as two especially lovely young women walked past ogling my athletic physique, further qualified my choice to pick this one. Whoever he was, he'd been far easier to enter than either of my previous bodies, not that they stood a chance to resist. But this guy was, to put it nicely, more brawn than brains. He didn't even have the strength of mind to be felt in the background. The others knew something was going on but this one just sat numbly, too stunned to protest. He was my second occupation this evening. I'd found to my surprise, that it was easy to put them on. Strange thing was once I was on-board it was like I wasn't responsible for anything that happened while in there. I took them for a test drive and slipped out when finished, leaving everything that had happened in that time a distant memory of something I couldn't be sure had even occurred. Was it all me, or part of my vehicle? Whatever I had done before donning my current apparel had been pleasant, but uncertain. I think it involved a date with a woman, but other than a lot of activity, thrashing around with that blonde woman I'd met earlier in the day, I couldn't exactly recall how it ended. I hoped it was as exciting for her as it was for me. I personally had the sensation of fulfillment in whatever we'd done together. Being relatively new at this, I hadn't learned how to retain all the experiences I'd had when I left my temporary home. Cursing the emptiness of this skill, I left my first body behind. Restless and not ready to return to Maddie, I chose this handy vehicle to check out the town in. The place Mr. Beefcake had walked into had a nice shopping area. Located on a central street, it seemed most people walked around and socialized in this location. My handsome shell fit right in among the young people posturing for each other; girls wearing skimpy outfits, boys showing their admiration for them, and me standing right in the middle of it all. For several hours I strutted around, just enjoying the feeling of being alive, even if it was only temporary. Reaching into this guy's pocket was also a pleasant surprise, he had lots of cash which I used to buy a large meal that included steak and shrimp, baked potatoes, French fries, vegetables, something called cheese sticks, chocolate cake and a box of candy. Food was something I discovered I missed more than I'd realized. I'll bet this guy was going to wake up with quite a stomachache, wondering why he gained a few pounds; I'm sure his physique wasn't achieved by eating this way. In the second I spent thinking of this, I decided his minor discomfort was acceptable because he'd live through it. Since I had discovered this great new way of playing, I planned to enjoy it to the fullest, even if the memory didn't stay long.

The longer I moved around, the less I cared that I still didn't remember much about my life, the feelings I'd begun to have when I followed my instincts far outweighed the blankness that followed. After all, I just had a wonderful evening, an evening I hoped would never end. I could walk around forever, eating, breathing, talking. Maybe if I never left him I wouldn't forget what I had done. Could I really stay here indefinitely living through him? I got an answer to the question a short time later. Sharp pains tore through *our* chest and breathing became difficult. How long had I been wearing him; I wondered as his beefy body fell to the ground. I felt his energy ebb until there wasn't much left to draw from. I guessed there was a time limit to the bodies usefulness, and since I hadn't really paid attention to the time since I'd switched hosts, I guess I'd better take what energy I could and go back to Maddie. He was gasping for air when I left him. Something inside me passed on regret as a crowd gathered to help him. Surely he would recover now that I'd released him. I moved down the familiar path towards Maddie while memory of my last conquest faded into pleasant myths.

Chapter Twenty-Maddie

I woke up on the floor remembering everything I had felt and seen, amazed I was still alive and totally me once again. The darkness and I had been so intertwined it was hard to separate myself from the horrible memories of what I knew had been her (whomever she was) death. Rising, I stumbled through what was now just my house. Making my way across the floor, footsteps hesitant, expecting to find myself back in the nightmare I'd just experienced, but nothing happened. The silence of the house was horrible, broken only by the squeaking of floorboards as I stepped on them, causing me to flinch on my short journey through my bedroom and into the bathroom beyond. Turning on the faucet with shaking hands, splashing water on the pale shocked face looking back at me in the mirror; I struggled to breathe. It felt worse to die as this woman had than it had been to actually die myself. Though I hadn't seen it all the way through, I knew her death had been the end result. Emotions that weren't mine clung to me like a second skin, still so strong I was having a difficult time recovering and becoming myself again. This woman had wanted to live so badly and was cheated out of that life by someone who had no right to end it. She hadn't been strong enough to fight him, so he removed her from the world with apparent ease, but not entirely. Her determination and will to survive in some way had caused her to linger somewhere just beyond my world, rage building, giving her enough strength to follow and attach herself to me like a leech waiting to make contact and suck all my energy out. What was it about me that, suddenly, every murder victim was seeking? I was pretty sure I could include Perry in the unwillingly dead category, looking young enough to not have spontaneously dropped dead on his own. However, it did seem strange that, unlike this woman who was solely focused on her time of death, he couldn't remember much beyond a few vague recollections about relatively benign things. Shouldn't he have retained the strong emotions of a person removed from the world unexpectedly. Maybe I had this wrong. What if he died in an accident, the trauma of it wiping out memories of the life he'd lost? I tried to think about what all this was telling me. It was hard enough to deal with a nameless person's grief and anger, but he knew me and wasn't likely to leave until he had answers. What if the answers were unpleasant, breaking open a floodgate of suppressed grief and resentment at his loss? You know what they say about being the bearer of bad news? Well, it hardly makes you the favorite person to its receiver. Seeking to calm myself, I let my thoughts go to my current situation. I was alive, and they weren't. Nothing that happened now would change that. They were merely remnants of something that used to exist, something that needed help moving on. I would help them and get on with my life. Keeping that in mind, I pulled further and further away from her experiences, putting them behind me like a bad dream. I was still alone, with no fear of her return and with each deep breath I took became angrier and angrier. I wasn't going to be anybody's puppet. She had no right to put me in that position. Neither did Perry who, strangely enough, still wasn't back. That was good in a way, since I needed time to get myself back together and be normal when he did appear. I had no intention of telling him anything that went on here. If I was to be confidant and counselor to these souls, then I should respect their privacy and not share information they passed on to me. I drew in another deep breath and stepped into the shower, quickly washing myself. I was fresh as a daisy, relaxed, and sitting at my computer looking at my messages when all the hair stood up on the back of my neck. Perry had returned. I didn't need to have his whispered hello echoing hollowly in the air to announce his arrival; every nerve ending in my body did that for me. Forcing myself to remain calm, I acknowledged his greeting with one of my own. Wondering why, for the first time since I'd met him, I suddenly felt afraid. Because the Perry that came to me now was different than the one that had left, and I wasn't sure why.

Chapter Twenty-One-Perry

She was sitting in front of her computer typing away as usual. I was pleased to see this, but she still didn't seem to have accomplished anything. When I asked how things were going, Maddie simply said she was waiting for information from a researcher she'd just started talking to. When I would have asked more, she asked me what I had been doing all the time I'd been gone. There was something about her tone and the look she gave me; eyes guarded as if she didn't want me to sense what she was thinking. I shimmered out of view. The answer evaded me. I didn't know how to respond. Flashes of darkness; a woman's face, mouth opened wide making sounds I couldn't decide were from pain or pleasure. The images were vague, random, unrelated, and not helpful to recreating my evening on the town. Hard as I tried, I couldn't separate the incomplete jumble of mostly useless information going through my head. People passing me in a large building, looking down from somewhere above. I also saw images of food, tree-lined streets, cars driving past, a strange room with flowery furniture, cheap wooden bookcases and worn tile flooring. Concentrating on the room to see what had happened there, I heard noises in the background, but still couldn't see anything specific. What I did see didn't occur in any particular order, randomly skipping past one moment in time to others I hadn't recalled before. Faces popped in and out of my head rapidly along with incomplete scenes of places I wasn't familiar with and couldn't make sense of. I mean, it was me and it wasn't; some of it seemed like things I might have done while alive but through someone else's body. I was living in reruns through another person, not knowing exactly what it meant or why I couldn't remember on my own. Uncertainty made me mute; I saw her eyes narrow as she honed-in on my silence.

"Where were you?" she said again, pronouncing each word sharply as if talking to a simple person having a hard time understanding.

Feeling compelled to say something to make her happy, I said the first thing that came to mind, "I think I was a carpenter." The statement came from nowhere, but I had a feeling that it was partially true. I don't know how that came to me, but in any case, she was surprised enough to stop asking the other questions and focus on this new information I was giving her.

"Did you have a memory?" she asked, her voice less guarded, body less tense, allowing her mind to go in the direction it should, the one I wanted it to.

"Yes," I lied, controlling my voice to continue the conversation. Well, it wasn't exactly a lie, I had remembered working with wood and metal at one point in my existence, just not if I had done it for a living or not. I knew I could do it and that might give her enough information to add to the nothing much I'd told her so far.

"I don't guess you came up with a name, state, family members or any other pertinent facts while you were remembering what you did?"

"No." The sound escaped my lips in the slightest of whispers. Thoughts of making her pay for using that tone with me had me mentally shaking my head. Where did that come from? This was Maddie I was talking to. She was good; I was good. I should be used to her personality by now; sometimes awed by me, sometimes annoyed, but always my connection, grounding me to this world. I hadn't seen or felt the dark thing since we'd stuck together. I was safe with her. She couldn't let me down. If she did, I would have to go back to the nothingness, and that was out of the question. I may not remember much about who or what I had been while alive but there was something left of me here and I was now aware that I could live again, even if only for a short time through others. Whatever I had been or done while alive needed to be remembered, completed. I had unfinished business. I felt it with an urgency and frustration of someone who'd been dormant far too long. It was at this very moment that I realized that I must have something very important to do for me to feel it so strongly. It must be why I knew I couldn't go into the light. The fact that I couldn't remember what it was must have had more to do with the amount of time I was gone. Now that she had woken me up, I'm sure more would come to me or she would find out for me. She was going to help me find it, finish it. I don't know if it was the tone of my voice, my refusal to show myself, or the fact that my presence had made the room so cold, but she didn't ask me anything else. I wondered about this because it was hard to get her to shut up when she was nervous. This was new behavior and I couldn't help but wonder at the change. As I watched her look once more at the computer, I was struck by her tense appearance, the slight tremor of her lips, the way her fingers hesitated for just a second over the keys. Could she be afraid of me? I was good, she had no reason to be afraid of me. I had unfinished business and that made me important. I repeated this several times to myself; a reminder of why I existed, why I had come back. I stayed unseen above her bed while she worked a little longer before she settled down to sleep, not bothering to speak to me at all. There was something going on in her head, but I couldn't tell what she was thinking. It was a long time before I knew she was asleep; breathing in and out in a relaxed way, the brilliant light of a living thing hovering so closely to her body. Watching her sleep, I savored the memory of her fear and tried not to ask myself why it made me smile.

Chapter Twenty-Two-Maddie

He'd had a memory; a carpenter he'd said. What on the surface had seemed an ordinary conversation was overshadowed by so many feelings. There was much beyond that simple statement that I couldn't begin to believe that was all he had been, because when he came back, it was as if he were a different Perry than had left hours earlier. I didn't understand the change any more than I understood his absences lately. The relatively predictable friendly lost soul had gradually begun to show himself as something a little less so, and I was reminded, once again, that I didn't really know who or what I was dealing with.

The sun was high in the sky and my parents long gone to work before I stumbled out of bed. It had taken me a long time to get to sleep the night before, what with my silent companion watching me like a hawk. I had pretended to relax while my mind continued its restless cycle of confused thought. Slowing my breathing to show him I really was deep in slumber, was all I could think to do to keep him from talking to me anymore. When my ghost friend had returned, I was shaken, still trying to put him into that comfortable, familiar category we had fallen into, when he once again proved to me this wasn't how our relationship was going to go. I had learned so much about someone I knew close to nothing about just by the way his personality changed from day to day. It seemed Perry had two sides, one charming and comforting, the other scary as hell. At times, I was dealing with an ordinary man who was eager to learn all he could about the world as it was now; sharing his view of the changes in customs and people from the little he recalled of his own time. These had been enjoyable conversations and I welcomed the new insight he gave to my era. Other times, he was a serpent, ready to strike when the wrong phrase or action was committed in his presence. I couldn't be sure when this would happen, and it set me on edge. But this last time was far different. The energy he brought with him made all my inner alarm bells ring. His tone was amiable, and he was saying all the right things, but as hard as I tried to pretend otherwise, I was terrified. Whatever he did when he was on his own had begun to bring out a bit more of what he once must have been, because he wore his new self like a well-fitting suit. The ease in which he conducted himself, fielded my questions, and lulled me into a false sense of general ok-ness made me question my own foolish assumptions about what I was feeling. I mean this was Perry, my supernatural friend, and he'd come to me for help. But there was another part of my brain that just knew there was something wrong about all of this and it was screaming at me in a way that refused to be ignored. At this point, all I wanted to do was solve his problem so he could leave and go on to whatever great rest he had to go to.

When I had woken up and failed to sense his presence I was so relieved I could have cried. I wasn't alert enough to play pretend with him right now. He must have gotten tired of waiting for me to get up and had gone off on one of his trips to the outer world. I almost let out a contended sigh but then the thought of the other thing that liked to visit me when he was gone had me stiffening up, holding my breath, and looking around the room for the darkness. I had no desire to experience that entity's last moments and didn't want to engage in a battle to keep it out of me either. The clock ticked by several painful moments of suspenseful dread in which nothing happened before I hesitantly rose and crossed the floor into the empty living room. A glance at the clock once again revealed it was after 4 p.m. Most of the day was wasted and Perry would be really upset when he returned to find I'd gotten nothing done. I grabbed a quick bowl of cereal and hustled to the mailbox which I found surprisingly empty. I went back into my room to grab my laptop. Flipping it on, I moved about, eating, washing my face, changing my clothes, and generally trying to present myself as if I'd been up most of the day accomplishing something so my otherworldly visitor and parents would be convinced I had not descended into depression and isolation. Now refreshed and ready to get something done, I browsed through my e-mails, saw one from my eager criminologist Dave and was just about to click on it when my phone began to ring. Crawling across the bed, I noticed there were several missed phone calls from Damen and here he was calling again.

"Hello," my brightest and cheeriest tone greeted him as if I had just skipped across the room after a pleasant afternoon spent lounging around with a glass of tea and snacks.

"Are you okay?" were his first anxious words to me. "I've been trying to reach you all day!"

"I've been working, turned my phone off and forgot I guess." The lie slipped out of my lips before I thought too much about it. I tried not to feel bad about that because I reasoned it would make us both happier not to have a conversation about my physical and mental well-being so early in the relationship.

"I guess you haven't heard the news then." His tone was relieved but serious and I knew something bad had happened.

"What news?" A short pause followed my question as Damen pondered how to tell me something unpleasant without sounding like an eager gossip. He was such a gentle soul. I knew he felt he needed to tell me this bit of information before anyone else did because it was something I would hear from others in a far less pleasant way.

"Jeff Samuelson is dead." It was a quiet, matter-of-fact statement delivered in a way designed to express sympathy and not sensationalize. The way he said it indicated there was more to be said but he wasn't sure how to say it.

"Jeff the mailman?"

"Yes."

"How?" My mouth went dry as I thought of the last time I saw him, when Perry had occupied him like a cheap suit of clothing, leaving only when I insisted he do so. Had this contributed to his death?

"Heart attack." Relief flooded through my body and I tried not to dwell on the fact that his death sounded so wonderfully ordinary. People died from heart attacks all the time, even when they appeared to be very healthy. For all I knew Jeff had some really bad habits that caught up with him. I mean, all those rumors about his womanizing might just have been the tip of a large iceberg of other vices. Poor man. Damen had continued talking and I tried to focus on his words even though my mind was far from this conversation, thinking only of all the reasons yesterday's events had nothing to do with his death.

"My partner and I found him after his neighbor called 911." Another pause, followed by a rush of conversation, "We worked on him for an hour but couldn't bring him back. I think he had been gone for a while before we arrived. We didn't know it was a heart attack at first. He was covered in blood. We thought maybe he had been attacked, but there wasn't a mark on him. It was strange enough that we had to call the police. When they got there, we were asked to leave." His tone told me there was still more to come. "I was worried about you, because he was at your house late yesterday, the neighbors told the police he was talking to you, and there's the woman they found not long after they found him. If it hadn't been for the fact that I saw your mother at the diner and she told me you were at home and perfectly fine, I'd have been over there already." All this came out in a rush as if he felt foolish or even more guilty for not coming to the house to see after me like he felt he should have. "When you didn't answer the phone..."

"Wait a minute," I broke into his long, tortured explanation. "Why would it matter that I talk to my mailman, and what does any of this have to do with some woman?" I guess he'd just have to spell this out for me plainly because the bits and pieces he was giving me were pretty confusing.

"I don't know her name, but they found some woman murdered and dumped along old Pickens Road. She was pretty cut up and there is speculation that the blood all over Jeff might be hers."

"What!" I shrieked. At the same time the doorbell rang, making me jump. "Don't worry, it's me," Damen's voice continued on the phone. "I couldn't stay away any longer, had to see you. Had to make sure you were okay."

I hurried to the door and swung it open it before being enveloped in a big bear hug from my frantic would-be boyfriend. "There is some talk about him possibly being a killer - and you saw him every day," Damen said between deep, desperate kisses. "I just had to know you were alright," he repeated before setting me carefully back on my own two feet in front of him, showing a remarkable amount of restraint. I knew he really wanted so much more to happen at this moment but was afraid he had come on a bit like a pro-wrestler approaching an opponent. I had to admit, with our chemistry building, I would have been up for more, had I not sensed we had company. But it wasn't Perry. I realized, to my horror, that the darkness hovered silently in the corner listening to every word we said.

I grasped Damen's hand for a moment, overcome by what he could not see before steering him to the kitchen to make a cup of coffee; retreating to neutral feelings while my unwelcome audience was present. To my relief, it didn't follow, and I listened while Damen told me the little information he had learned of the sordid tale unfolding in town.

"He had pictures in his spare bedroom. Disturbing ones of women." Damen's face was pale as he recounted what his friend had told him. "Pete wouldn't have told me this if your picture hadn't been there too."

I blanched at this statement, horrified to learn that my friendly mailman had been someone different than what I'd suspected. The pictures showed injured women and one of them was of me passed out in my hospital bed. I remembered Jeff stopping by to visit, but didn't remember him taking a picture. Damen kept a tight hold on my hand as he swore me to secrecy. I was to act surprised when the police came to talk to me. We spent an awkward hour sitting together after he dropped this startling information, with me trying to process this latest bit of sickness to enter my life while expecting the darkness to follow into the kitchen at any second. And poor Damen, thinking this was the only thing I had to deal with. So now I had known a serial killer and two dead people. I wondered if Perry had sensed this about Jeff while he was in him and, did the heart attack have anything to do with his recent possession? I had to talk to Perry. There was so much I couldn't tell Damen. I wasn't free to pursue anything long as these things haunted me. I realized now, more than ever, that I couldn't encourage him any longer; it would be cruel. We weren't alone and would never be until I took care of this situation. It wasn't fair to him. We concluded our conversation with me telling him I appreciated his concern, but I was alright and planning my departure from this town soon. I lied about a job offer in another city, before he got the chance to tell me he loved me. I sensed that coming and knew it would break my heart to hear; I mean he was fairly screaming it to me through his eyes and I couldn't ask him to deal with the baggage the dead had brought to me. If the building activity in my life was any indication of what was to come, I couldn't put my parents through this either. I had to be far away from them all as I dealt with this messy situation. He left soon after, with red eyes and a hurried step, head down, not once looking back. He made it all the way out to his car and down the road before I burst into tears and turned to see the black blob hovering in the doorway to the living room.

Chapter Twenty-Three-Perry

I found myself by the sign down the road from Maddie's house again. She was asleep, and I couldn't wake her, so I took the time to explore my surroundings. Not having to sleep myself, it was helpful to make use of the time to orient myself to the living world again. Every time I took a body, though I couldn't remember much about what I said or did, it brought back a little of myself. I hadn't told all of this to Maddie. I was hoping to find out more about myself as a person. I knew I was good, I just had to be able to tell her that. Memories filtered back of working at a desk, so I must have been a professional man. I saw a calendar with the days marked on it, meetings penciled in with times and dates and names I didn't recognize. My hands writing things out, picking up a large telephone receiver; the lovely girl I remembered from high school days smiled at me from a photo that sat on my desk. I wished I could recall her name. She was obviously important to me; why couldn't I think of her name? Seeing her face brought out the strongest feelings in me: passion, love, guilt, regret and sometimes anger, but I could never remember her name. I had little time to consider the reasons behind this because these memories were quickly replaced by others. Sometimes I would be sitting by myself in the dark, excitement making my heart race, watching people walk by, thinking of things I could do. Thinking of secret things that made me happy, the things I didn't have to share with anyone else because they would never understand. Every man had vices, I'm sure they couldn't have been that bad, maybe I liked to drink or have some quiet time away from everyone. I was a good person, I just knew it. I had to have been. Everyone I saw in my mind had seemed to really like me. Smiling faces always greeted me, showing confidence and genuine delight. I was a good person. All the things I saw around me were nice, quality things so I had to have been successful. Hard work and success were all markers of a good man, I recalled that much about my era. All the visions I saw from my life were good and that told me I must have been a good person, making me wonder what I could have possibly left undone to wander around avoiding the light for so long. There was something. There had to be something I had not quite finished for me to have delayed my departure from the nothing. It couldn't be that I liked being in the nothing. No, being alive was so much better, and lacking that, the use of a living being was an acceptable substitute for the actual thing. I had enjoyed the sensation of walking on solid ground, feeling lungs move air in and out, touching objects. I was sure I would get much better at retaining the experience as I went along. At least until I got the answers I sought to move on, of course. I would move on, because I was a good soul, wasn't I? That's what good souls were supposed to do. Whatever was happening while I was in these people was becoming quite addictive, making it harder and harder to resist but I supposed I could do it when necessary. After all I was a good man, I was sure of it.

I had just convinced myself I should return to Maddie's house, make her tell me what she had found, when I noticed, with interest, Damen's car moving slowly away from that direction. Through the window, I watched his tear-stained face stare straight ahead, unaware of my presence. I wondered what happened to make him so sad. I could feel sorrow hanging around him like a second skin. I breathed in his dejection; it was like an open invitation, a beckoning call to taste his weakness, to take advantage of his unguarded, vulnerable state. Had he been his usual jovial, self-confident self, his body would have been hard to invade. It seemed this type of person was more resistant to spirits such as I. I would have known instantly if I wasn't welcome, but as it was, he practically screamed an invitation to me. It wasn't my fault. He was there and in his state of mind, there was no way I could resist taking advantage of what was offered. It had been only one day and already I missed everything life had to offer. She wouldn't miss me for a while yet, and well, whatever had happened between them would not have her missing him either. No man cries without great reason. I had a feeling this is how I might have reacted to the dark-haired girl's loss if it had happened to me. Sometimes love makes a man weak, and I was sure that even though I didn't remember her name, or much about her, I had loved her. Maybe if I took this man in love for a test drive it would stir up memories I needed to move on, or at least hold on to memories of the things I was doing while I was occupying him. Reasoning all this out, I accepted the excuses I gave myself and slipped into Damen, promising myself I wouldn't stay long. I owed Maddie that much. It would be okay; I'd send him back to her soon enough, maybe even with a solution to their problem. I was a good man. What could go wrong?

Chapter Twenty-Four-Maddie

Huffing and puffing, I stood out in the yard, glad my parents weren't home yet to witness my strange behavior. I had waited until Damen was gone and sprinted from the living room as fast as my legs would carry me. I wasn't sure if that thing could follow me, but it hadn't tried. It merely hung like a fine mist, visible through the open door. There was no way I was going back to experience her death again. Just because I could see and hear ghosts didn't mean I was willing to let them traumatize me at will. I had to draw the line somewhere. So, leaning awkwardly against a tree, I engaged in a battle of wills with the dead woman's spirit. I didn't want to think about the fact that I was completely alone in all this, had just pushed Damen away and would soon have to do the same with my parents to keep them out of it. I had gotten confirmation of my insurance settlement from the cow's owners, which would give me the opportunity to move out and become an adult again, an adult who could talk to all the ghosts she wanted to without anyone thinking she was crazy. As soon as I talked to the police, pretending I didn't know all that Damen had told me about Jeff, I was getting the hell out of here, leaving this town, memories of my death, and all my previous failures behind me. A quick look at my watch told me my parents should be home soon. I couldn't stay out here forever, I'd have to go back inside and present a sane front for them. Taking a deep breath, I crossed the yard and peeked cautiously in. Sensing nothing out of the ordinary, I allowed my feet to cross the threshold and stand for a few minutes of uninterrupted aloneness. Roaming the house like a burglar expecting the owners to arrive at any minute, it still took twenty minutes of creeping around to assure myself I was indeed alone. Shaky legs carried me back into my room to find my computer still on, e-mails showing on the screen just as I had left it. Well, almost like I'd left it. One message was opened, the print enlarged on the screen to five hundred percent, so I could hardly miss seeing it. It was from my partner in research, Dave. Since I was sure I hadn't done this myself, I couldn't help but wonder why this message was so important. Sitting down to read what he had wrote, anticipation made my fingers hit the keys with the finesse of a thick fingered monkey. What followed was a series of warning beeps after which the screen flickered but stayed on. Eagerly reading the much awaited communication from my new friend, I hoped to learn something amazing to explain my dark stalker's interest in it. Dave started by saying he appreciated my asking him to participate in this interesting exercise in crime solving. He wondered if he could use it as a case study for his class. Sounded reasonable to me, as long as he gave me some information I could use, I didn't particularly care what he did with the results afterwards. It could hardly matter to Perry since he had been dead so long and I had no vested interest in this situation beyond having him move on. After weeks of searching databases for untimely deaths of young men in the 1930's, Dave was excited to report the discovery of a man who had died tragically on a highway near a state park in Virginia. He went on to say that he was impressed with my drawing, stating that it looked a lot like the photo he had attached of the deceased. Clicking on it, I found myself staring at a grainy, gray image of Perry's head which, ironically, looked much like how I saw him anyway. It was hard to tell what the exact cause of death had been just by looking at the picture, which had been made basically for identification purposes only. The autopsy findings were included in another attachment. Markings on the male outline figure showed several wounds on the torso and legs. The notes accompanying it told of impact injuries consistent with being struck by a car. No report of a hit and run was ever received. No one came forward with any information regarding the man or his death, so the case was still technically open even after all these years. There had been blood, and lots of it. Understandably so, considering he'd been hit by a car; but some of the blood hadn't been his. Forensic science was still relatively new at the time, so all the medical examiner could tell was the blood type and that there had been more than one. Other than that: nothing. Since DNA testing hadn't been available at that time and no other body was found, its owner could not be identified. How this man got where he was found was a mystery; there was no mode of transport immediately obvious in the area. Maybe he'd hitch-hiked, but there were no witnesses to confirm this. After months of circulating his picture in the newspapers, not one person had come forward to identify him. Poor Perry. What happened to you? This was so frustrating, because now I knew what had happened but not why, and still didn't have a name to give him. Maybe sharing the cause of his death would make him remember. This is what I was thinking when I turned to find the darkness hovering over my shoulder. Shrieking in alarm, I fell back, scrambling away from it before gathering my wits to stand my ground. - If standing my ground meant remaining on my feet but in a low crouch, ready to bolt at any second, because that's what I was doing. A low moan, not mine, filled my ears as I concentrated on keeping this thing out of my head. To hell with Miss Friendly, conduit to the other side! I knew I was not going to experience the horrific memories of her last day on earth again. There was no way she was going to make me! We were face to face now, me staring into a blank void where parts of my room had been. My space had been invaded by a solid mass alternating between a complete random mess of thick goo, to something that tried to resemble what looked like a woman. From the center of the mass, eyes blinked, and lips moved, gasping out icy puffs of air toward me. Goosebumps broke out all over my arms. As the face before me formed and reformed, she seemed to be trying to say something but all that came out were anguished moans. Air swirled around me. I was again reminded of our last encounter in her cold memory. I know I once had the idea that I was some kind of ghost whisperer, helping lost souls like an intrepid hero in the movies, but it seemed I could only tolerate Perry. While I tolerated him less than before, he scared me far less than she did. She came attached with far more need and strong emotion than he did, and I couldn't help but wonder why he seemed to remember so little about his own traumatic death while she hadn't forgotten a second of hers. What was it about them that made their tragedies different? And how was it that they both picked me to haunt? Part of me wanted to let her in but I was too afraid. I pushed back at her, forcing her away while my computer screen went crazy behind me. I heard electronic beeps like someone was typing furiously, making mistakes but continuing despite them to get the message through. Partially turning, to keep one eye on her and one on my computer, I watched as words formed at a furious pace on the screen.

The words *Let Me In* typed repeatedly on the screen followed by different words. *Killer. Must. Be. Punished. Accept. Responsibility.* Did that mean me? I watched in amazement as words continued to show up on the screen without benefit of hands. *Be Careful. Don't Trust. Can't Rest. I'm Lost. Look for the car.* Fascinated by the dead woman's messages, I almost turned away from her. A slight shift in the air reminded me of my mistake. I stumbled backward, narrowly avoiding the approaching mass while increasing my mental resistance to it. The cloud hung there for a second or two more before breaking apart at the sound of the front door opening and my mother's voice calling my name.

Chapter Twenty-Five-Perry

The human me was tired and breathing heavily. This was the third day I'd been away from Maddie. I hadn't intended to stay away so long, but since the day I'd learned how I'd died something in me snapped. I'd waited all this time to find out I was a successful, popular man, only to learn I was an unidentified body on the side of a road. I'd come back to her house after testing out Damen for an hour or two, pleased to note that I'd been able to recall most of the time I'd spent driving around in his car looking at the town, the people, some with more interest than others, and visiting a drive-through food place (an awkward but useful experience) only to return to discover the obscure details of my demise. She'd showed me the photo her friend had sent, which I recognized as my own lifeless body, along with a report of the injuries I'd died from. I still couldn't believe it. How could this be? How could I have been left as a nameless corpse with no legacy? This could not be right! I was a good man. There had to be more to my life than this. Maddie said she planned to contact the police in the jurisdiction I was found. Maybe they would have more information. But that wasn't good enough, damn it. I hadn't heard what I wanted to hear and then she asked me about the mailman again. Had I gone back to him? NO! I'd screamed at her.

I had no memory of visiting the mailman a second time, and that was the truth. Then she told me about what he was, what they had found out about him. He was a killer. That explained some of the strange things I was remembering. I got the impression that she had considered, just for a moment, that I might have something to do with his death. I was very angry and confused, and I guess I over-reacted. When I had left her, there wasn't much of her room left intact, including her precious computer, which I fried pretty effectively, putting all my renewed energy into it with lethal results. I could hear her cry of dismay as I sped out of her room, leaving the smell of burnt electrical equipment behind me. Someone had to know what had happened to me and she was taking too long to find them. Then I realized how long I had been dead. The chances of anyone who'd known me surviving that long were slim to none. One roadblock after another and I had things to do yet! I felt it stronger day after day, the longing to complete a task I'd started long ago. She was my human connection. I was drawn to her. But maybe now she wasn't so necessary.

After all, since she hadn't really found out much for me. I had others I could use to complete my task. I was certain the longer I occupied them, the more they could help me remember. The first time or two didn't work out so well. I hadn't been selective, not paying attention to the aura surrounding the form I slipped into. My energy level was low. I just wanted to live again, so I took the first person I found alone. I had sensed weakness; that's what drew me to the man. But thirty minutes after I moved into him, he had an asthma attack. It was very traumatic for me to be caught in a man who couldn't catch his breath; shame too, I had planned to use him to test my longevity. I'd been forced to slip out before his attack affected me too greatly. Looking down at my gasping transport, I moved on, after vowing to be a bit more careful with my selection process, hoping the man I left behind would recover soon. What if I picked another killer? I had to think of that too.

Having occupied a few less than desirable shells, I reminded myself to look for the little clues to viability, any hint of the brown haze of illness or evil that would make me have to leave quickly was not acceptable. They couldn't be too young either. I was a good man. Children were definitely off limits. So, I told myself, only good, strong men were needed for my purposes. Damen had been perfect. I had left him far earlier than I wanted to, but only out of respect for Maddie. I would have worn him again, but finding the same person more than once was harder than you would expect. It could be done, but they weren't as easily tracked as Maddie; it took a lot of energy and I couldn't waste my limited time unless the result was worth it. I used what I could find, even spending the night in one of them, right next to his wife. I liked being there, even though she noticed something strange about him, lying as far as she could to her side of the bed. When I tried to touch her, because it would have been fun to try sex as a living man, she pretended to be asleep. It didn't bother me too much; she wasn't much to look at anyway. But the point is, I remembered it all. Every second of it, and he was still sleeping quite soundly when I left him. I then moved on to a man walking past my uneventful encounter's house early in the morning; a quick transition of available hosts. After a day and a half of body hopping, it was getting easier. I was able to remember many things I hadn't been able to before. Well, of what I was doing while in them, but not one thing about myself. How the hell was that! By the second day, things started to look up. I was having dreams. Well, maybe not really dreams, but something like them. They were my thoughts, not his. I didn't allow him to have his own thoughts. I was the one in control. I had to be. He was my vehicle. I put him in a relaxed state and let my mind wander, like floating in the nothing, but with scenery. I was walking in the school hall again, smiling faces passing me, whispered words in my head: "I love you, I'll love you forever." Each word made my heart hurt because I felt she had meant it, but had done something to ruin it. Whatever had happened to me had something to do with her. Why did I have the sick feeling that women were a large part of my problems? Was that why I was dead? What had I ever done to deserve death? Her face was in my head again. Why couldn't I remember her name? Her face so pure, so beautiful, kissing me, eyes shining. I knew she loved me. She wasn't faking that. So what had happened? What had gone so wrong?

My borrowed hands were shaking as I sat forcing memories to the surface. I was talking to her. We were arguing. She was crying. I wish I could remember more. I tried to hold the memory of all I was seeing. I was running. It was very dark. I was scared. This couldn't be happening, wasn't supposed to be happening. I had to stop this. It was wrong. She should understand. She should know me better, understand that I loved her. Struggling to stay in the moment, I tried to see what happened next, but the scene changed, and I was talking to someone different. Red lips, smiling white teeth, mouth moving, always moving; I didn't know what was being said but it bothered me. I'm not sure what would have happened because random memories took over once again and I was walking down the hall, greeting smiling people, opening the locker, picking up textbooks. Hands working on wood and metal, endless repetitive tasks which ended in me running in the dark again, and then nothing. *Our* hand slammed down on the wooden surface in front of me. It hurt, but I savored the pain because I felt it. But it didn't restart the memories. Frustration left me restless. I walked down the street in search of a distraction, I saw it in the form of another person. His feet moved as I directed them. Together we followed the object of interest into the deepening night.

Chapter Twenty-Six -Maddie

Pacing around the hotel room I'd occupied for two days now, I tried to relax. I was getting so tired of pushing the darkness back. It had managed to get into my head the few times I'd fallen asleep, treating me to first-hand experience of running away, breath coming out in terrified gasps as she tried to show me the last few moments of her life. I woke up, terrified and full of rage, both at what she was doing to me and my inability to protect myself from her while in my most vulnerable state. This whole situation was pissing me off! After Perry tore up my room the other day, I was too shaken to stay. I wrote my parents a note after hurriedly cleaning up the mess. I stopped by the bank, cashed the check I'd just received from the insurance company, purchased a used car, and left. I didn't have time to go through the motions of long- drawn-out goodbyes with explanations and a lot of back and forth-ing between me, Mom and Dad. I hadn't even stopped to do my civic duty and speak with the police about Jeff. He may have been a killer but he was dead and to my relief, so far had not tried to contact me from the great beyond. If I sensed him at all, I would block him, a feat I'd only mastered while awake. It was my dreams I had to worry about, and little to no sleep was my new routine. If I was trying to distance myself from the dead, I was doing a horrible job because Perry stayed in my mind despite his absence. Strangely enough, my travels took me on a route directly toward the state park in Virginia where Dave had said Perry was found. I looked it up and followed the directions on the crime report from over eighty years ago, going as far as to locate the Sheriff's office of record. It wasn't as easy as it sounds, because you would be surprised at how much changes over time and, unlike some of the movies I'd watched, there was no one on the police force the least bit interested in traveling down memory lane with me about an incident that happened so long ago. The officer at the desk was less than impressed with my research story and had no further information to give, but he did allow me to make copies of the reports on file. I believe his exact words were, "It's an old case, so no one really cares." So here I was, exhausted, in a strange place, wishing I could just get this over with. I found the hotel. It was a bit of a flea bag joint, not filthy, just raggedy, and old. I was drawn to it instantly; no doubt because it was cheap, and I had to make my money last awhile. It was late by the time I returned to my temporary home from my waste of time at the police station, the small file I'd copied clutched in my hand, ready to study the attempts that had been made to identify the dead man and his murderer. It seemed his photograph hadn't been circulated as far as it could have been, and so it wasn't surprising that Perry had gone unidentified. Beyond the few small towns surrounding this area, no one had actually seen it. It seemed the Sheriff, a man named Adam Richardson, had been close to retirement. After failing to get results from his meager attempts, he put the incident down as an unfortunate homeless man crossing the highway at the wrong time. The case remained open, but with no hope of being solved. From the notes in the file, it was clear the Sheriff had considered the disappearance of several young women in the area over the previous few years his top priority. He had not solved those cases either. Judging by the question marks and swear words written in the margins, along with a few random notes that didn't exactly apply to Perry's death, he wasn't happy about it. Wonder how this stuff wound up in with Perry's. Sloppy record-keeping, I guess. My eyes were blurry. I put the file down, and started up the new laptop I'd been forced to purchase after Perry's tantrum. Coming up empty on his situation, I tried to find a little more information on the missing women that had occupied so much of Sheriff Richardson's time. I typed in the name of the local newspaper and looked up old stories regarding missing persons. I was pleasantly surprised to find a series of articles spanning two years. One story had a photograph of a woman that caught my eye. She was beautiful. I could tell that much even from the small, fuzzy likeness they had placed to the left of the story printed on Page Seven. I don't know why, but she looked familiar. She was missing, I mean, had been missing all that time ago, but hadn't been important enough for the front page. My head was dipping downward as I struggled to stay alert and process the information I had found. Why was I having such a hard time reading the damn words?

I had a vague impression of observing myself from above, face planted on the keyboard before the scene in front of me changed. I was now somewhere else entirely, walking in a hallway, people smiling at me, talking to me like I was well-liked, going to a locker and picking up books. Closing the door, I saw a good-looking boy smiling at me, a boy that looked a lot like Perry. Then I woke up.

Chapter Twenty-Seven-Perry

I was so satisfied with myself. I had been through four hosts and had total recall of all the time I'd spent in the last two. I hadn't wanted to leave; this last man had been quite comfortable. While "in borrowed flesh" as I liked to call it, I had acted quite normally, visiting people as a passenger, learning a whole lot about my surroundings. Watching people had been quite useful, moving among them even more so. I had begun to think about what I was, and could have been. But other than a few memories of mundane daily activity, I couldn't remember anything specific. I did know I could build things, liked hamburgers a lot, was athletic, and that people liked me. I was a good man. The few things I could recall played in my head repeatedly, like a pre-programmed loop. Memories teased me until I felt like screaming. I knew I was a good man, an important man. I just needed conformation, something to tell me that I was right. I kept seeing her face; laughing, crying, but always stopping before I could witness how the scene played out. The only clarity I had was the present and what I was doing in the body I was occupying at the time. Why in the hell could I not remember anything significant! Frustration overcame me. My temporary hand slammed into the wall next to me repeatedly; the pain helped me focus. Bones snapped. It hurt like hell and I was shocked to see the hand below me become swollen and red, blood flowing out of the cuts I had created with my actions. The face looking back at me from a mirror on the wall looked disgusted. I felt awful for doing this to him. His distress was evident even in cloudy, unfocused eyes. I should set him free. Pictures of him posing with his girlfriend who had walked away from us in a very uncomfortable state after speaking to him for an hour reminded me to pick a loner next time. After all, I was a better man than this. I wasn't cruel. I'd just needed a body and he had been available. It was an opportunity I could hardly pass up. But now I was all messed up inside. Nothing was going as I wanted it to go. His emotions kept coming through, making everything worse. I felt his exhaustion, pain and confusion. I needed to leave before anything else happened. I was the cause of all of this. Hanging out here wasn't doing either of us any good, I couldn't bring up any recollections of my own identity while dealing with his emotions. I was still a stranger to myself and I knew that in my current state of mind, I would do more harm to him if I stayed. I didn't think I'd be able to stop myself from hurting him. This is not what good people do, and I was a good person in bad circumstances. I knew it.

What I thought would be a solution to Maddie's role in my search had turned out to be so much less. Taking a deep breath, I admitted to myself that I did need her, after all. I couldn't stay away from her any longer. No doubt I would have to do a lot of apologizing for overreacting the last time I saw her. She would undoubtedly be very upset with me for tearing up her stuff. I hope the computer wasn't too difficult to replace. I needed her, and she would just have to let me back in. We had a connection. She had an obligation to me and I wasn't going to let her forget it. I reminded myself that she had at least learned where and how I had died. We could start from there.

Ironically, the non-believer in ghost stories that I was wondered briefly why I wasn't haunting the place I had died. Didn't ghosts usually do that, haunt the scene of their final tragedy? I slammed my head against the wall in frustration, fuming that I had once again remembered a useless fact. Control was leaving me fast. The rage built up over centuries of dead and forgotten existence was making me react in a very uncivilized way. Wearing people was no longer a pleasurable pastime, but an exercise in futility. If I was going to use these living people, and I most certainly planned to, I needed to learn who and what I had been and how I could accomplish my goals. I had the opportunity to finish whatever I had started. The urge to do this had built up so strongly I wanted to vomit. It was like a pressure within my soul that I just couldn't deny. I had to be strong and in control of my destiny. Life had ended too soon for me. My mission had to be completed, whatever it was. Unsated hunger gnawed at me; that big empty space which used to be me needed to be filled once again. I wasn't going to waste more time like this. It was important to move on, to find my link, my solution to the mystery of me. I exited the body I was in, leaving him falling to the ground, holding his hand and groaning in pain. Flying far above the sight of my injured companion, I felt remorse. I was a good man, after all. He was moving toward the phone to call for help as I left him. Assured all would be well, I went in search of the pretty lights that would take me to her. Only when I tried to find her, she wasn't where I'd left her. She was far away, in a place I had strange feelings about. A strong sense of nausea and dread moved through me. I had to have been from around here. I'd died near here, so why, other than a strange itching in the back of my mind, was there no instant revelation about anything? Damn it! My energy quivered in frustration. What was it about my life that I couldn't recall anything beyond useless junk? With renewed determination to learn about myself and what my life had been, I sped toward the glimmering light that was Maddie.

Chapter Twenty-Eight-Maddie

I woke, dripping in sweat and wondering why I had seen a younger Perry in my dream. What did the woman have to do with my personal ghost? The cheap clock on the worn bedside table told me it was 3:00 in the morning. I was alone and couldn't sleep. Suddenly I had the strong urge to look a little deeper into the disappearances of the women that had so obsessed Sheriff Richardson.

I started my search with a map of the surrounding areas, looking up every article from the 1930's that pertained to missing women. After hours of reading the newspapers and the late-sheriff's notes, I managed to find eight unsolved disappearances that matched the names in the deceased lawman's files. Of the eight, I was able to verify that all seemed to have been blonde except for the last one, the lovely brunette woman whose photo I had seen before falling asleep. I read a few of the descriptions about the other women. They were relatively ordinary; missed by few, and it seemed, quickly forgotten. But the last one, she was different. Her face stared back at me from its place on the screen underneath a short article about her loss and those who missed her. Her name was Sierra Glenn, a grocery store clerk from Wheeling, West Virginia who, to all intents and purposes, no longer walked among her loved ones after January 15 of 1937. She wasn't incredibly important as far as income or contribution to society, but she was missed by her family, and that family happened to have known Sheriff Richardson's wife. The connection was close enough that she had appealed to him to investigate her daughter's disappearance. I read the letter her mother had written, expressing her heartache and strong desire to find her daughter. He never did. But, according to his notes, he had talked to law enforcement officials in the surrounding states. He had even gone as far as giving her information to the local paper to write a story. That's when he noticed the other women. There were more notes in Perry's file that pertained to the missing women; it was strange there was almost more information on them than on the dead man he was supposed to be investigating. There was a map in the folder marked with dots and the name of the women, indicating places they'd last been seen last. And right next to Perry's name was a big question mark. There were smaller, unmarked circles near the dots, with small symbols, their significance long lost with the death of the man who'd made them. While I had originally considered him lazy, not committed to finding Perry's identity, he was obviously very involved in finding out what happened to these women. Amid the chicken scratch of random information, I was able to make out the words *I think they're dead. Bodies?*

Why did he have all this junk in one file? Why did he think all these women were dead? What proof did he have? Why did all the paperwork stop exactly one week after Perry's body was found. Richardson certainly was cryptic even though I was sure no one bothered to read his notes anyway. I'm sure things went no further than the secrets he held in his head, things he apparently didn't want to share with others. Whatever he did or did not discover was either not in this file or somewhere else, somewhere I did not have access to. I felt like Alice in wonderland, where things just got curiouser and curiouser. My world was about as nonsensical as it could be. I was scared and tired beyond reason, but didn't have a chance to think about doing anything beyond putting the papers away as I sensed a familiar presence rapidly approaching. Perry had found me and I didn't want him to know what I'd discovered. Gathering all the paperwork together, I shoved it into the folder, put it under the mattress, turned on the television, and waited for his familiar form to appear. I didn't know what to do or say, so I put on my best neutral, *what- the -hell -are -you -doing- here* expression. I couldn't tell him what I'd seen or that the memory seemed to come from another entity. The darkness was trying to communicate with me, but I didn't understand what it had to do with my ghostly friend. Was it because they were both victims? Or something simpler I had sensed in him as I was dreaming, and he randomly became part of my vision? This was getting confusing. I wanted to go back to sleep and get a little clarity but couldn't. I was awake, confused, and not able to show any of this to my unshakable dead companion.

Weakness was not something I could share with those who might make use of it. I still wanted to help him but wasn't quite sure how much I now trusted him. He'd said he hadn't gone back to Jeff's body, that part I had believed. I felt only sincerity when he said he didn't remember being there. From what I'd managed to read in the papers the past few days, Jeff had been practicing his little hobby for years now. I couldn't help but wonder if Perry had gone back into him, maybe he could have stopped that last woman's death somehow. Perry may be a little scary at times, but he was good, manipulative, but good. It must have been something else that was bothering me. I'd been through a lot lately and so had he, but that didn't excuse what he'd done or how he'd acted.

Memories of what he did to my laptop were still fresh in my mind along with his scary personality when he flipped out on me. He had been gone for days and part of me hoped he would stay away, while another part still wanted to help give him peace. That nagging doubt kept me on edge, wanting to believe I was doing the right thing, the noble thing. If I was just able to get him to move on, it would be alright. Anger and fear were in my head, fighting with mercy. I know you can guess which instinct was winning. Here I was, doing his bidding, stuck in events that had occurred long before my life had begun. Too involved in something I had never intended to get this close to; it was becoming very complicated. The room became cold as he shimmered into view, smiling at me like charming Perry, apologizing for what he had done the last time he saw me.

"I was just shocked by how I died," he said with just the right amount of remorse and boyish regret. "I would never hurt you," he practically purred in my ear.

Perry was just as he had always seemed, but for some reason every hair on my arms rose up in fear. A tiny little voice whispered to me from a source I like to call instinct, that told me to close my mind to this connection, keeping him from reading my thoughts or sensing the things I was thinking. All he could see was what I let him see. (Yes, I had gotten that good at protecting myself, at least from him) Days of dealing with the darkness reminded me of how I was constantly at risk and I had enough presence of mind to push back aggressively. She may have been able to get through a time or two, but I was going to make sure that didn't happen again.

Cautiously, almost nonchalantly, I rose from the bed and moved away from his grainy form to the bathroom door. "Where have you been?" The first words came out rough and gravely as I shook off the remaining sleep and concentrated on letting him see only good old Maddie doing what he wanted her to do.

"Looking for myself, trying to remember who I was and why I died," he said, without actually telling me where he had been or what he had been doing. "I thought I could remember without you. I was wrong about that."

Hovering in midair, he continued to watch every move I made. The intensity of his stare creeped me out a bit as I stretched my legs and tried to act like normal Maddie.

"Well, isn't that nice!" I snapped, recalling quite clearly how he had trashed my room and computer. I pushed back at him with an energy borne of resentment and desperation. My strong response made him shimmer in and out of focus for a second, his imposing presence became uncertain once again. He began to feel more like old Perry, the one who'd shown me how desperate he was to learn his identity and fate. The atmosphere was clean now, not disturbing at all and I was comfortable enough to sit in the chair by the door and face him with renewed confidence in my safety. My newly formed safeguards still well in place, I waited for the inevitable question.

"Did you find something? Is that why you're here?"

Chapter Twenty-Nine-Perry

The air around me vibrated with an urgent need to remember a mission I had yet to complete. I felt warped and stretched out. She was here and looking at me from across a ratty hotel room with an expression I didn't quite understand. I was sure she had sensed me arrive before I revealed myself; our connection worked that way. I knew it, counted on it, and had made the most of it. For the most part, she acted like her old , dare I say, bitchy self. I seemed to have that effect on her from time to time. I can't say that I blamed her, considering what I'd done when I last saw her. I acted charming and apologetic, trying to show her how sincere I was and how much I still needed her. I took it as a good sign that she had managed to find her way to this location; it meant she hadn't given up on me despite what I had done to her. I was a good man and worth the effort; I just knew it.

She was *here*. I was almost certain I should remember this place, the place I died. I knew it, mourned it; every tree, stone and dirt road in this area held a clue to what had happened to me. These objects had witnessed my demise out on some remote stretch of highway and I was still clueless as to why. Yet the emptiness of my past was beginning to crack slightly. I saw glossy, goo covered lips smiling; admiring eyes shining at me. It was just a quick thing but stirred up so many emotions; I was mad, strong, fearful, in control and yet oh so lost; contradicting myself at every turn. I was a good man, so I couldn't be all those things at once. Small details were falling into place, resulting in confusion. I was a good man but sometimes felt the need to be away from all the things that made me good. I think I drove a lot, the road called to me with the promise of freedom. Maybe I had been unfaithful. Maybe that had been my shortcoming. It all came back to women. Had she been jealous, this woman, was that why I saw her crying sometimes? It didn't seem to me that it could have been anything else. I was sure I had been very good to her otherwise. She had really seemed to love me. Memories of how she had looked at me stayed with me long after death; the adoration, her kisses, the feeling she could do no wrong, along with the sick feeling that maybe she had and that's why I was dead. I don't know why I felt this way or why I was angry about women in general from time to time. I never stopped to think about it before. The strange images of things I wanted were coupled with disgust. The blonde in the hallway so long ago, one of the few things that stood out besides her obvious wickedness was the contrast in feelings between the woman with dark hair and the one with light tresses. One evoked amazement and adoration, the other the deepest disgust, primitive feelings I didn't want to admit to. The thought of a certain type of woman was unpleasant to me, bringing to mind images of the worst kind. They made me angry, filling me with a longing I had no right to have. That's when it hit me: these feelings were part of who I was, or had been part of how I saw them.

Of all the things I didn't know about myself, the one thing I was beginning to realize was that I did not like blonde women. I did a short mental inventory to assess my feelings on this matter; there was no middle ground on this issue. It, for better or worse, was my closely held certainty. This deep internal knowledge wormed its way out of my head and came out as a truth I was not sure I wanted to know.

Okay, so everyone has their own thing. I put this down to the morality of the time I lived in. It was all neat and tidy in the 1930's, right? There was decent and not decent. I had the impression of being raised on this concept. After all, it made sense to me in a way that only someone who had known this all their life could possibly know. It must have been my parents. I wish I could remember them but sadly, not a single thing occurred to me on this matter. I must have loved them, that's how you feel about your parents, but I couldn't remember them at all. Every recollection revolved around me, what I had seen with my own eyes, and that dark-haired beauty. Strange that no family ever came into view. I was raised well because I knew I was a good man, so I had to have had good parents and a strong value system. What stuck with me was the fact that I associated a dark-haired lady with purity and redemption, and brassy, light-haired women with something different. They were artificial and showy in a way I found very distasteful and undignified. What bothered me was the fact that I sometimes desired these distasteful, undignified women and was sure I steered clear of them because of it. It was all I could do. After all, I was a good man and that's all I would do, right? I told myself this over and over as short chaotic scenes played out in my head, things I didn't understand but dreaded. Red painted lips smiling at me mockingly, laughter, moans, whimpers. All this followed by feelings of the deepest sorrow. At first, I assumed it was because of

112

something I had done, but it couldn't be. I was a good man. It must be whatever happened between the dark-haired woman and me. I believe she hurt me deeply. Maybe we had argued. Noises and crying, a faint scream ringing in my subconscious. I think she failed to understand who I really was, how good I really was. I also think we parted ways, leaving me heartbroken. I should hate her, I know, but think I still loved her. Whatever was left of my humanity mourned the loss of what we had; all I had to go on were emotions with no clear events to accompany them. Maybe my amnesia had to do with whatever happened between us. I wondered how her life had gone after we broke up. Did she miss me? Did she regret the dissolution of our union? Whatever had happened between us, happened just before I died. I was hurt, angry, wandering around in a fog, more and more convinced with each tick of the universal time clock that it all came back to her. Too much time had passed. If I could just remember what occurred, maybe I could forgive her and move on. I was reasonable after all. I held on to the one thing I knew had to be true: I was good.

Pictures in a magazine, perfectly dressed people, perfect cars, perfect life, perfect woman, all flipping past at a furious rate, fought with images of another kind. Sitting in a car, anticipation of finding just the right thing at the right time, heart racing so fast it hurt, squeezing my thigh to keep from acting too quickly. Flickering lights, then darkness, headlights, clean leather seat making a creaking sound as I changed position, hiding evidence of my arousal. Many trips *here* to a quiet hotel room out of town, hoping they didn't think I visited too often. "Can I give you a ride?" Destination: grassy field. My favorite spot. I loved this place. It was perfect. I guess I wanted to show her. The need to make her understand what she thought she knew…

All this vanished almost as soon as it came to me. Then there was just Maddie sitting in that chair looking as if she might bolt out of it any moment. Like that would have done any good. I couldn't let her go now, not when we were so close. She would give me answers and I would find peace. My soul became still at that thought and I could see she felt it. She settled back into the chair with a renewed sense of comfort.

"Find out who I was," I pleaded with her, a final tug at her heart strings. Nodding, she looked at me with eyes I couldn't read, mind and thoughts closed to me in a way they hadn't before. Accepting her assent, I tried to be satisfied with the moment of forgiveness and her promise to solve the mystery of me. A niggling sense of another influence in her life hit me for just a second and I wondered what it might be. Had she been browsing through her ghostly encounter books again? Did she think she knew something about how to handle me? Small things about her demeanor; fear tempered with determination and a vague hint of authority to keep me at bay.

"I need to get some sleep," she said, glancing at the clock next to her. I saw that it was 6:30 in the morning. Without saying a word, I let her lay down and waited next to the bed for her to wake up while trying to decide why she seemed different, and why this building had a certain feeling of familiarity to me. I was content to wait for her to wake up, occupying my little section of the room, when I saw him out of the corner of my eye, the recently deceased form of a weak and damaged soul hovering just above Maddie's head.

Chapter Thirty-Maddie

I woke to find him still there. The bedside lamp didn't work, but he seemed hazier than usual after he sucked all the energy out of my stuff. At least his presence had kept the darkness away, giving me a chance to sleep another couple of hours without fear of dreaming someone else's tragedy. But there was a moment last night in which I was sure I had felt a slightly familiar presence lingering in the back of my mind, just enough to give me pause. I looked carefully in every corner of the room, just to assure myself that Perry and I were alone. When I failed to feel or see what I thought I remembered, relaxed and put it down to stress. The form I'd seen standing next to my bed, his mouth moving without the benefit of sound, couldn't have been real. Surely, Perry would have sensed him too. But, his behavior didn't indicate anything was amiss, in fact, he even seemed friendlier and not as demanding. If Jeff had truly been here, I'm sure he would have raised the alarm.

"Good morning," he said pleasantly.

He was too nice, like he was being careful to say just the right thing to me. Now that raised alarm bells.

"Anything happen while I was asleep?"

"You snore." His answer was short and to the point. Adding a "How do you feel?" to the statement to soften its effects.

"I'm fine, what time of day is it?"

"Afternoon," the soft reply floated on the air. "What are you planning to do now?"

I felt impatience radiating through the air, and something else. A certain something I wasn't sure how to take, a barely contained excitement that made the room shimmer with a life of its own. Whatever Perry had been revealed itself slowly but surely in the form of subtle, barely restrained emotions. I didn't know if he was even aware what was happening. Perhaps it was just his eagerness to move on but the more I saw of him, the less sure I was that he would be satisfied with just that.

A soft sighing sound hit my ear. I felt him next to me stronger than I ever had, almost as close to life as he could get without an actual body. I smelled a musky type of cologne and the warmth of exhaled breath hitting my cheek. Every hair on the back of my neck rose in protest. Whether intentionally or not, Perry had invaded my personal space in the worst way. Much like a living person standing far too close for comfort, his spirit was seeking to connect with mine on a level I wasn't comfortable with. I think he was beginning to suspect that his wasn't the only soul I'd encountered.

"Have you seen *It* lately?" he asked oh so casually, as if without a second thought.

Moving to the other side of the room, I stood in front of the mirrored cubicle by the bathroom door, forcing myself to brush my hair one slow stroke at a time. This girl is not scared, see?

"*It*?"

"The, dark thing," he pronounced each word as separate and distinct, something that needed to be understood and taken seriously.

"No." While I rarely ever lied, I felt compelled to answer in the negative in response to that little voice urging caution. I swear I almost heard the word "don't" in the lowest level of my gut as if she, my dark, dead companion resided there.

So with a straight face I turned, looked at him and again said, "No," feeling, for a second, stronger than I felt before. I wondered where that came from. "I haven't seen *It* since that time when I was dead."

"Maybe something like it then? Something unpleasant?" Once again, feigned disinterest in my answer, just a soft, monotone assemblage of words, seeking something specific without offering a reason. He was being extra weird and creepy today.

He stayed where he was, staring at me with cold black eyes revealing nothing of what he thought. With a flat smile, he popped out of sight like a broken light bulb. Just a quick bright flash and then nothing at all. He must have seen me shake my head no; I knew he was still close by because he spoke again.

"You'll still help me, right?"

"I'll still help you," I said. There was an awkward silence for a moment before I continued. "I noticed that the Sheriff who found you has a grandson in the area. Maybe he has some information." I actually had seen that while looking at the deceased law man's obituary during my early morning research. While it was a long-shot, it might be enough to get a little more information about the man doing all the investigating into those girls, and why he spent so little time on Perry's case. Eager for a distraction, I grabbed my laptop and started it up. Looking intently at

Adam Richardson's obituary, both to find the correct name and avoid further conversation with Perry, led to identifying Luke Richardson, Adam's only living relative. A few minutes more and I had a local address and phone number to go with the name. A short conversation with the puzzled man had him agreeing to meet with me that day. Finding the address on GPS, I felt my stomach rumble. I grabbed my stuff and headed out the door toward the small diner located next to the hotel.

"Where are you going?"

A nod in the direction of the eating establishment was all I could do while hotel employees moved about cleaning and keeping the old place from falling completely apart. I had managed to appear normal enough for someone who didn't seem to have a purpose for hanging out in this out-of-the-way establishment, but they were curious nonetheless. I didn't want them to see me talking to myself like a crazy woman. I know word had gotten around that I had visited the police station, so they were now sure I wasn't a fugitive. Still by the speculative looks I was treated to daily, I was sure I had been the subject of many a conversation regarding why I was *really* here. Being the occupant of one of three booked rooms, the other two having arrived just last night, I was sure I had been here longer than most whose car hadn't broken down on the way to some other place. Being close to the state park no longer mattered here as there were other entrances closer to the main highway.

I wasn't even sure why I chose this place. I mean, I could have gone the traditional route and stayed at one of the more popular places, but I just had to come here, to this hotel.

Strolling into the eatery, I sat and ordered a meal as if I didn't have invisible company watching me eat every bite. So, we were back to the constant observation, me silently enduring his perusal and he, impatiently occupying space. I didn't so much enjoy my meal as much as just fill my stomach out of necessity. Hastily finishing my sandwich, I got in my car and headed to visit a man who might be able to help. Amazingly, Perry did not follow. I felt when he stopped being *there*. He hadn't given any warning, he was just there one second and not the next. There was a slight tingling on my skin as if something in the air shifted near me, then nothing. I didn't feel anything unusual and I did not feel Perry. Not sure whether to be relieved or alarmed, I drove on toward my appointment with Luke Richardson, hoping to get closer to the truth that would set us both free.

Chapter Thirty-One-Perry

I had vowed to stick with Maddie every step of the way, learning everything she did about me on her visit to the Sheriff's family. But as she moved toward her car, I had a sudden change of thought prompted by the presence of something or someone new. My attention was captured by an emptiness in the air, like something that had once existed was struggling to be seen again, to occupy space. Though weak, the force was trying to form and be acknowledged. I wondered briefly if this was part of Jeff's spirit again. I was sure I'd dealt effectively with him yesterday, putting as much negative energy toward that sneaky little bastard as I could, letting him know this was my living person. He couldn't visit her like this, and would he stop putting his memories in my head, because I was now sure that's what was happening to me. My brief contact with him must have carried over somehow. Ever since I borrowed him, I'd felt things I couldn't have felt while alive. No good person sees women the way I saw them recently and knowing what he really was, I naturally attributed these new memories to him. It was a relief to know this. He was a spiteful, evil, soul, laughing at me when I said this, but I pushed him out easily, he wasn't strong enough to stay then. What about now? I had to protect Maddie. Sorrow and pain, on a level far below anything I had ever sensed, stained the atmosphere; fuzzy and fearful but determined to emerge. Impressions flashed into view like lightning, sometimes brighter, sometimes dimmer, first in one spot then another. A glimpse of a face at times in front of me, sometimes behind, moving in a way only a spirit could. Here I was in the living world feeling as if I were back in the nothing, what with all the dead company I suddenly had. I couldn't see the soul clearly, but the emotions it put out were enough to catch my attention and make me want to see more. The energy lingering here called to me with an urgency to be heard, strangely filling me with a sense of superiority. Maybe it was because I was so good at this and whoever it was, was not. I really felt strong and proud. Why? The energy, already inferior to begin with, shrank back from me after giving a quick glimpse of light hair and wide eyes. The form that was attempting to emerge then moved away at a high rate of speed. Naturally, I felt compelled to follow. It was like hunting and I think I liked hunting, it felt comfortable, like a well-rehearsed and often practiced hobby. I was having fun; my heart would have raced if I still had one. As I moved through the atmosphere of this world, chasing my elusive prey, I sped past trees and through a few isolated buildings, an insubstantial form passing through posts of rusty steel and rotting wood, stopping only when another form caught my attention. Residual energy from someone different hovered around me, flitting from tree to tree, trying not to be seen. It too carried a hint of fear and determination, but was different from whatever I had been tracking before. The energy was different. It was aware of me, watching with interest but hesitant to get too close. Maybe I had known it or experienced something with it, but couldn't catch up to find out. Then there was yet another something a little further down the road. Cloudy remnants of life appearing teasingly in the distance, all bringing up thoughts of excitement, revulsion, and authority on my part. I moved closer, only to sense a new presence this time even further down the road. Abandoning the last cloudy form as it disappeared into whatever the beyond was, I sought out this new thing and followed the trail, this time catching the faint scent of jasmine hanging in the air. The odor brought back memories of great pleasure and guilt. I had done things, things I didn't want known. It must be as I was beginning to suspect; I was a cheating dog. Maybe that's why I parted with the dark-haired woman, but I couldn't be sure any of it was my fault. After all, I couldn't remember much about her except the impression that she had betrayed me in some way. This must be why I remembered this place the way I had, it made sense that I would stay in an out of the way hotel like this. I was a good man with a weakness; I had to accept that, but it wasn't a reason for me to die. I was a good man. I WAS a good man! Another filmy form flirted with me from yet further down the road. I followed, memories of my car moving slowly down roads just like this, being oh so clean and careful because I was a good man. I must have no tickets, no hint of scandal. This place was far from home, I stopped at the sudden realization that this was a significant memory. It caught me so off-guard that I wavered in and out of view, finding myself in the nothing again.

I screamed in protest watching the world I had just been in from a milky entrance, the shady images I had been chasing watching me with interest, venturing closer to the portal. I counted five separate formerly living beings lingering in the woody area I had just left. Eyes blue, -gray, green. stared at me, the only distinguishable features in the hazy blurs they displayed. Each set of colored orbs bought a different feeling with them: fear, regret, anger; but they all seemed to know me. I couldn't say the same about them, the only emotion they stirred in me was pride and power. I was the one in control, had been then and still was because I was a good man! Anything I had done was justifiable for reasons I had yet to discover; It was something I had always known, would always know. I was a good man. Someone had always said that's what I would be. Looking from the outside in, I savored this new recollection. I let it seep into me, hoping to fill in the blanks with the total knowledge of who I had almost remembered. It didn't come. Then it occurred to me that I was dead, had been for quite some time. Shouldn't I have met some of my family or at least a few acquaintances? Why hadn't I connected with anyone from my past? I thought when you died there was supposed to be spirits of your dead relatives waiting to greet you. I saw that in some of Maddie's movies yet I was always alone. Why was that? Turning my attention from the living world, I scanned the gray place once again, with this new idea in my head.

Blurry things passed me here as they always had, at a high rate of speed on their way to whatever their destiny was. Strange that I had never discovered mine as I felt so many souls here had. Some had moved rapidly toward the light, or toward other blurry things. I was isolated with no compulsion to seek out anything, or anyone, in particular. The only thought in my head was that I didn't want to be here and, given what I now knew was possible for me, didn't need to be. I had the ability to live again, so hanging out here, hiding from those things out there was an insult to my superiority. Anger, a potent emotion, still lived on in me, like memories of love. It was just as strong now as it must have been when I was alive. The souls here were dead and powerless. I held the secret of renewal and rebirth. So what if it didn't last as long as I wanted? I was getting better at it, and with each life bits of who I was returned to me. I planned to move back where I belonged, in the living world and claim my destiny, finish my mission. As I moved toward the opening, the forms on the other side moved back, shrinking from me, fear echoing in the air when I sprang forward to continue this merry chase. Their figures beckoned teasingly. Anxious to overtake them, I paid little attention to the area behind me and was surprised to feel myself quickly encompassed by another long dead entity demanding my attention.

Chapter Thirty-Two-Maddie

Driving into Luke Richardson's driveway was a good, lonely experience. Perry never had returned, his disappearance was abrupt and unexpected, leaving me quite puzzled. I couldn't think what would have made him leave like he did. It didn't make sense. But come to think of it, as this whole situation went on, it made less and less sense. But at least I was truly alone. No dark woman. No Perry. Just me, a bright sunny day, and a pleasant drive with the radio blaring to some catchy tunes. When I finally reached my destination, I stepped out of the car with a smile on my face, totally relaxed, and was met by a nice-looking older man with white hair. Ushering me into his small white house, Luke Richardson listened intently to my reasons for wanting his grandfather's old records. I told him about Perry's death and my project to find his identity. He nodded, seemingly amused by my interest in an event that happened so long ago. I got the impression he thought me a little silly, but was willing to help me nonetheless. Now that I was here, I was very curious about the man who'd shown such interest in the missing women but so little in the death of the man I had come to know as Perry. Luke, as he insisted I call him, talked about the Sheriff with restrained respect.

"He was a serious old man," he told me, eyes lowered. "I don't mean to say he was mean or anything like that. He was a wonderful man who loved his family very much. We used to visit a lot. His daughter, my mother, lived down the road and she was very close to both he and Grandma. Grandma was very open and easy to read but Granddad, he always seemed to have something on his mind. Reserved is what I'd call him. He didn't laugh often but I remember I always felt safe with him; he took our welfare very seriously. He died when I was sixteen, just after I got my driver's license. I didn't have a father around, so he helped me practice until he was convinced I was ready to be on the road with other people. He was relentless about my knowing just what to do; making sure I was prepared for the test. He took me out on some of the less traveled backroads to practice and when we got to one particularly out of the way road, he always got real serious; I would say kind of scared and sad at the same time. Strange that it always seemed to be the same spot, a deserted area just on the edge of the state park. I don't know why we even went there since it bothered him so much, but we managed to find ourselves there every time. I don't know why I think this, but he might have visited this place more often than that. Grandma did say sometimes he would get quiet and disappear for a while, coming back in a strange mood. He'd hug her tight, tell her he loved her, then go into his study for a few hours to look over paperwork from a job he was no longer doing. She never intruded on his privacy, but said files were often open on his desk when she went in to clean up, even on the day he died." Luke stood for a moment then produced a photo album from a desk behind the couch. Flipping through several pages until he came to the picture of a tall, thin man with dark-colored hair, wearing a tan uniform. In this particular picture, he was smiling, and I didn't get the feeling of a very serious man. He appeared quite approachable, his attention caught by the person taking the photo, the focus of his smile.

"My Grandma always said that was one of her favorite photos. She took it before he left for work one morning. I think he was in his forties then. They were so much in love; I could always tell that by the way they acted together, always holding hands, hugging even as they passed in the hallway. It was a good thing to see, especially after my own dad died. That love was security to us all. He was a bright man who took his job seriously but could also have a good time with his friends. That's what Gran told me. I don't remember all of it, just that he was my Gramps, the steady guy who kept me out of trouble."

Turning the pages of the album past collections of children's parties and various family gatherings, he stopped at a picture taken of his Grandfather a few years before his death. He was standing next to a younger version of Luke, his expression sterner, less open than his previous image. Maybe it had to do with the mood he was in the moment it was taken, but he did seem different than the man who'd posed a decade earlier.

"Over the years he became more guarded and a little sad. She always wondered why. I remember talking to Grandma shortly after he died. It gave her comfort to talk about him, felt it brought her closer to the man she loved."

Luke showed me a picture of a short woman with curly blonde hair standing next to a younger version of the Sheriff. Judging by their attire, it was their wedding day, both were smiling broadly for the camera. She was lovely in her simple white dress, a bouquet of flowers in the hand placed against her husband's chest as she embraced him. Then, as with his Grandfather, presented an image of her later in life. Still lovely, looking sadly at the camera as she posed alone, palm placed on the empty space on the couch beside her.

"She lived to the ripe old age of ninety-five, outliving my mother about twelve years. Great women, both of them." Luke smiled sadly, closing the book, and placing it on the table in front of him.

Clearing his throat, his thoughts returned to his previous line of conversation. "Gran did say she thought the change in Grandad started after the disappearance of one of her friend's daughters. She had asked him to work on it as a favor after the family was dismissed by their local police force. He didn't know them so well, but if Grandma asked, there was no way he would ever refuse; he would do anything for her. The girl's family had been told she was a young woman who, after spending her life in a small town, most likely packed up her things and ran off with a man she had been dating. This was in the 1930's, a time when people could, and often did, disappear and re-invent themselves, but her mother said she had a feeling in her gut that this was not true. So, when this friend appealed to Gran, she was willing to do what she could to help."

"Did he ever find the girl?" I asked, curiously, for his benefit, because I already knew he hadn't. This whole experience had made me quite the actress since I couldn't share my real agenda with anyone besides the dead. Maybe when this was all over, I could turn over a new leaf and be open and honest about all the strange things I was experiencing. Maybe share it with someone who had a little perspective about this type of stuff. I thought about Damen, missing him terribly. I made my mind shut up as I tried to catch up with what Luke was saying. Stress and guilt made my brain babble to itself again and I missed a little of the conversation. So, wide eyed, I attempted to catch up, hearing the words midsentence.

"...looked a long time for her, months," he said, pointing to an old newspaper article he'd produced from another book. It was the same article I'd seen online with the grainy picture of the dark-haired girl I was now sure had shared her death with me.

"Are you okay?" He had stopped speaking and studied me with concern.

"Oh, I'm fine," I said, smiling to assure him. Sipping the glass of water he'd given me earlier, I tried to appear interested, encouraging him to continue.

"He lived thirty years beyond that, but Granny was sure something had happened during that time that changed him; she felt it in her heart." Luke took a breath, pausing as if to gather his thoughts. "I'm sorry we got so off track, I thought you were here to discuss the man who was found dead on the road by the park." Even as he said this, his considering glance told me maybe he had been talking about what I really wanted to know the entire time. But I was here for Perry, wasn't I? It was important to find out about him, not the woman I was slowly finding myself more and more curious about. Her situation had caught my attention now that I had been treated, first hand, to her tragedy. Drawn into her story by default, I might have stayed there, braving further contact with her to end this once and for all, had he not returned to become a disturbing and persistent thorn in my side. Hell, I was so scared of both of them, it would be hard to pick which one I wanted to leave first. While continuing to appear focused, I thought briefly about my life before all this crap happened to me. Normal seemed so far away. Letting out a mental sigh, I pulled out a copy of Perry's picture for him to see. It was a copy I had printed from the autopsy photo with all the gross stuff cropped out.

"Well, I did look into his files after you called and found a few references to this case in a notebook. I read a few of his notes but didn't see much other than his having sent the photos to some towns around here." After a slow, searching glance, I was treated to a brilliant smile after which the handsome older man handed me two folders. "You are staying in town?" he asked as my fingers closed over the material. I paused uncertainly for a second, afraid to say the wrong thing lest he change his mind and take back what he was kind enough to show me. Silly thought, really. He seemed so nice and I just couldn't imagine him changing on me like that. I hoped I had read him right, people could be different when they wanted to. Look at my mistaken relationship with Joe. Well, no, I sensed he was no good for me but at the time it seemed kinda exciting. I had promised myself that was the last bad decision I would make. Only look at me now! Smiling sincerely while silencing my stupid thought process, I nodded my head. "At a hotel just outside of town."

Luke nodded too before he let go of the precious written material he was entrusting me with. "Good, because I'm trusting you to return them to me before you leave the area." The paper contents in the folders crinkled slightly as I shifted them in my lap, setting them there for a reassuring second in which I strove to show him I wasn't going to bolt out of the house now that I had what I'd come for.

"I can make copies and return everything to you in the morning, if you are alright with that."

"No," he said quietly, his features shifting for a second until I felt I was talking to a more friendly man. My skin tingled in a distressingly familiar manner as the perceptive ability death had given me kicked in to gear. I was suddenly facing a serious, sharp-witted man who saw so much in my eyes. Every move I made told him something he wanted to know. I got the impression of a skilled interrogator with years of experience, and I had to fight the urge to call him Sheriff and confess everything. This was Luke, but at the same time, not Luke. "I want you to know," he whispered softly, so softly, in fact, I wasn't even sure that's what I heard.

The whole encounter, brief as it was, ended with my facing the same pleasant gentleman who'd engaged in conversation with me for nearly an hour; a helpful soul who simply continued the conversation with, "I trust you. Just be sure to return them before you leave. I'm sentimental, I guess. Grandpa always loved finding answers, I get the feeling he would have helped you if he could." He made this last statement with a slightly puzzled look on his face as if he'd said something he wasn't quite sure he'd meant to say.

"Were you a policeman too?" I asked,

"No, I taught school for many years. I don't think I could have done what Grandpa did. He was so good at his job. Very good judge of human nature, I always heard."

I nodded, trying to shake the feeling of unease I had felt earlier. He was already a different personality, open, gentle, with a trusting nature, just like when we first met.

We spoke a few minutes more; I left him my number and the name of the hotel I was staying at with a promise of keeping in touch and returning the materials I'd borrowed as soon as possible. Then, with a polite farewell and offers of thanks, I pulled out of his driveway and down a few streets into an empty parking lot, suddenly eager to read the file while I was still alone. It couldn't wait until I reached my room. I felt there might be some things here I didn't want Perry to know.

Chapter Thirty-Three-Perry

As she moved through me once more, sickly sweet perfume surrounded me. Jeannie, the sad little blonde tart had found me again. Whispering words like "I missed you," and "Where did you go?" Enticed and repulsed at the same time, her presence sparked a feeling of superiority and disgust long repressed, but I suspect, always there. It occurred to me that she had been something I might have played with for a short time and moved on, just like all her other men. Maybe that's what drew her to me, the familiarity of the situation. This sudden change of thought shocked me at first because I was a good man, too good for the likes of her perhaps, but she wouldn't soon forget me. Instincts were awakening as she intertwined her aura with mine, hoping to reconnect as she had on our last encounter. Only this time I wasn't as anxious to leave as I had been before. I had a different thought. What if I stayed joined with her, and showed her just who I was? The thought made me smile; I felt her draw back a bit at the change in my aura. While initially the fact that I had been a man was a big draw to her, the change in my attitude seemed to give her second thoughts. I felt her essence shrink from me, the glossy red smile I had been treated to, slipped a little.

"Why are you so different? You were empty before, now you…" The feminine spirit seemed uncomfortable with whatever she sensed in me now. For some reason, it made me want to stay within her cloudy mist and explore this new part of my personality. This part felt so far from lost; almost like I was slowly slipping back into myself, or whatever I had been. This powerful insight into what made me who I was, may have once been, didn't so much bother me as make me smile. I had learned I was in control when I was alive and that wasn't a bad thing. I wasn't wandering around without a purpose, I was a strong, independent man who had commanded respect. They did what I said and made me happy after which, I went back to my home, carrying on life as I had before with the knowledge that I was a clever man, untouched by my hobby.

She saw it now. I wasn't just one of those men she thought she could control. I was so much more. Whereas before she had been clingy, now she was struggling to separate herself from me, to be anywhere else but here. I didn't understand why she was afraid. After all, she was dead and so was I. Seeing her just as clearly as I had before, I noticed a frown on her beautiful, heavily made up face, as she looked at me. It made me pause for just a second. I was a good man, but it bothered me that I was glad of her fear. We were locked together a few seconds more, me and her weak trembling soul; she really was ridiculous. With a sneer of contempt, I released her. She wasn't worth my time. She had nothing to offer me in regard to my past, beyond the fact that this little encounter showed me a little bit more of myself. Her blurry form, now freed from our entanglement, flitted quickly away and into whatever section of eternity she chose to settle herself in, or could be she wandered around endlessly in search of Mr. Eternal Right. It was of no consequence to me. In fact, I wasn't sure why I was here again experiencing what I was sure had to be some of Jeff's memories. It must have been his personality she sensed, it was a shame that the only thing I'd managed to retain from my experiments in living were bits and pieces of a killer's personality. I'm sure I could leave these him behind as soon as I found out more about myself. Was that why I was here? I had been pulled in; that hadn't happened before. And I could see windows I hadn't seen the entire time I'd been here. These openings were different from the time I had sought Maddie. Glowing a dull gold color like one might see with the setting of the sun, they drew me in like a beacon I couldn't seem to resist. I moved in the mysterious way I always had in here, each second brought a little more clarity as I was guided to the opening closest to me and entered.

The room I found myself in was alive with activity, people were moving about placing food on a table and laughing, none of them seemed to be aware of me. It didn't really matter, though, because there was something beyond them that I was seeing; they were just secondary images, a minor distraction to my memories of this place. I had lived in this house. There was a different layer here, one that occupied space beneath the present ordinary timeline. The living people faded away and I was looking at my past reality, one that still existed in a mind long slumbering. Arguments, a long-suffering marriage, a lonely woman, a preoccupied man, a young boy adored by both. Poor Mother, he fools around, you know? More love given to the boy than was perhaps comfortable coddling. He was a substitute for all the rejection she suffered and all the frustration the man felt when dealing with her. The boy wanted for nothing except stability, but he made it work for him. He got everything he wanted and was able to strut out into the world feeling it owed him something too. Smiling, always smiling, people felt they knew him, watched his confidence, and wanted to be part of his ride to someplace wonderful.

Hovering above a table filled with people I didn't know, I watched another scene in which a small boy sat through a quiet, tense dinner with two adults barely speaking. Each bite of food like saw dust to his taste buds. He attempted to fill the silence with stories of his wonderful day. The woman smiled at him; the man smiled at him, but the feeling in the air was all wrong and this went on for years. Endless years of togetherness that was more a matter of proximity rather than emotional bonding, with him being the glue that kept this all together. Adoring her, scared of him, it went for the longest time. They grew older, he grew older and saw things, less than flattering things, about them both.

Hanging there above the memories, I watched what I sensed was my own miserable young face transposed over the present scene for a second before knocking over a plate and shooting off as a mist past several shocked faces. I was back into the gray nothing for a whole second before being catapulted into another opening. Like all those other times, I was, once again, moving down a hallway toward the all familiar locker, the noise of voices all talking at once in the way people do when they are young, full of energy, and gathered together in one area. Pats on the back as if I had done something great that everyone knew about. Clothing from a former decade, my decade, and people as I remembered them. And a name over and over, "Hi, Jimmy! Good job, Jimmy!" They liked this Jimmy, had no idea what this Jimmy was really like inside, a determined young man with a very defined sense of right and wrong. So very proud, knowing so much that they did not. I knew this was me, was how I felt. I had a name now, Jimmy. Locker front, books, all like before, beautiful girl there when I closed the metal door. Words whispered so only I could hear, "I love you," then she was gone, and seconds later, so was I, despite a strong desire to stay and finish this scene. Though it had happened so long ago, I still felt that love. I was convinced it had been real, but I didn't even remember her name. Above it all, my spirit moved over the crowded parking lot that had once been a school, the phantom remains of which existed only in my memory. Not sure why, after all these years I was being treated to a suddenly revelatory run-down memory lane. I hadn't even needed to have Maddie for this. I had found out more about myself in a matter of seconds than I had all this time hanging around this woman who was supposed to be my savior. I hadn't found out anything really bad; I was still a good man as far as I could see. It was going so well for me now that I didn't mind the pace at which it was happening, it was long overdue. At this rate, the mystery of my life would be revealed, and I would soon be able to move on to something better.

Anticipation made me flow willingly with the mists transporting me through my past, what I had seen was good, surely there was more. My attitude changed in the next instant when I was taken from that place to another more confusing one. The last minutes of my life came rushing at me with full force and I was left gasping in shock and outrage. Feet running from a dark field to crunchy gravel, observing more than feeling, as flesh and bone met steel, body crumpling in a heap, numb realization that I was dying, spirit trying to hang onto a useless shell. It was at that moment I realized that it wasn't me who needed Maddie, she needed me. I turned from the place I'd seen my life end, to the person who stood on the road and watched as the last of my blood seeped from my mortally injured body and the rattling of my labored breaths stopped sounding in the still night air. I knew when I died. I had even hung over my killer's shoulder, watching as he quietly opened his door, official gold star and seal of the Sheriff's department on the side panel visible in the dull gleam of the car's interior light before the man slowly pulled off down the road.

Chapter Thirty-Four-Maddie

I held the pages with trembling fingers, reading notes written by a man long dead. Most of the information I had in front of me was about the missing women. A very thorough man, the Sheriff had a short biography on all of them. All different, from all walks of life. A down-on-her-luck prostitute, waitresses, shop girl, one unemployed woman named Ginger, two aspiring models and, of course, the cashier, Sierra. I noticed from the photos he had collected, that all were blonde, except Sierra. The women in question had a habit of partying, if witness reports of their character were true. From his extensive notes, it seemed like the Sheriff had spent a lot of time going to the surrounding towns asking questions about women *who had just decided to leave* their small towns. Most statements he'd received from those he interviewed were followed by the question of why did he care. These women hadn't had many ties to their community and, sadly, no one was too concerned about their absence. Sierra was the odd person out. Not particularly important, but different enough to be the red light that caught his attention after he was asked to look for her. As a regular person, I might not have connected these women together but Adam Richardson had. He had given all of them a great deal of consideration, as evidenced by the amount of work he had put into investigating them. It looked like he had gone from Sierra to the others in a backwards timeline; the only shared trait being that they were gone, never to be seen again. Among the things he had created to organize his investigation was a crudely drawn map with each woman's residence on it along with last places they were seen before disappearing completely. A different colored dot for each person showed just how methodical he had been. Facts meticulously recorded on several sheets of paper outlined a case that apparently went nowhere. I saw the word *bodies* with a question mark next to it scribbled above a circle that encompassed the state park not far from here. Re-reading through the facts of each missing woman case, I had not found anything to indicate that these people were dead. None of them were ever found, yet the number of times I saw the possibility of their bodies being somewhere near here came up repeatedly in his notes. I made my best effort to read as fast as I could, wanting to find something that would help me identify my ghost friend before he showed up again. Why did I have all this and yet nothing about Perry in a file Luke had handed me when he wasn't really Luke?

This experienced lawman had obsessed over a case he couldn't prove even existed; no victims, no villain, nothing except a suspicion that something bad had happened. Why was I still looking through this? It was obviously a waste of time and wasn't getting me any closer to helping Perry. Flipping impatiently through page after page of detailed notes, I stopped when I saw Perry's autopsy photos clipped to a few loose pieces of paper. The small collection looked out of place among all the other things in the file. I was drawn to it, hoping to find the reason for its placement among the missing women's information. Not willing to look at the pictures again, I removed the clip and placed them face down with what I had already gone over before turning my attention to the five pages of notes that went with them.

Millie Stapleton said he stayed here often, the neat handwriting informed me. There were dates and times referring to the very hotel I was staying in now, the name of which was written in the margin. *I find that interesting since no one is sure what he does while he's here. He registered as John Smith,* the heavily underlined name with the word *hah*, and an exclamation point next to it. Who was he referring to? Had I come across yet another case crammed in among the two in this file? Did Sheriff Richardson have some kind of policeman's ADHD? This brief moment of puzzlement was soon solved when a small photograph slid out from beneath the papers and onto the seat next to me. It was Perry standing next to a blue truck, his figure was small as if taken from a distance, but I knew him immediately. Tall, slender, and dressed in cotton slacks, with a casual jacket over his white shirt. The living form of my specter was parked in front of the hotel I'd been staying in. I expect he had no idea he was the focus of a law man's attention. The more I read, the less sense it made to me. The Sheriff had to have known who Perry was. He had seen him when he was alive, and had been watching him for some reason. Flipping the photo over, I saw the initials J.D. heavily underlined as if this were something Sheriff Richardson had known but didn't necessarily want anyone else to understand. Why would all the other information he'd gathered have been so clear and precise to the point he couldn't go any further with it, and then suddenly, become so vague when it came to Perry's identity. This was crazy!

With the picture still clutched in my hand, I read on; the thin sheets of remarkable information sliding against each other while I absorbed the contents. There it was, a detailed timeline of surveillance that stretched out for months before Perry's death, even before Sierra's disappearance. Perry had been here many times, the staff all reporting he went out late at night, often coming back to his room in the early morning hours looking tired but otherwise the same as when he had left. The staff was incredibly helpful and very interested in the man they saw every few months. He had supplied them with an interesting subject of speculation, but other than that, there was no proof of any wrongdoing on his part. Perry's visits didn't connect in any way with the disappearance of women or any other crime for that matter. Cryptic notes and dates joined to each other by dashes and brackets failed to establish any kind of pattern of criminal activities on Perry's part, other than he came here a lot. Yet Sheriff Richardson seemed to be indicating he thought otherwise and was trying to prove this as he went along. Missing women Perry was never seen with but who the Sheriff seemed to think knew him; women he'd never found, but seemed to think were dead. Was I dealing with a militant law enforcement Nazi bent on making Perry or *J.D.* a scapegoat for a fantasy crime? The initials indicated he had a name to go with the face, so why had he written Perry's death off as an unidentified case, unless *J.D.* stood for *John Doe*, then it made perfect sense. But I had a hard time believing a man, seemingly this thorough, would have given up before he knew it all. All these questions swam around in my head until I got to the second to last page of the notes. It was then that I realized I had been reading the pages out of order. He had been interested in Perry because of his being out of place, but merely as a possible criminal element poaching, theft of natural resources, illegal moonshine stills operating in the middle of protected land. These things happened in the state park often enough to make him keep an eye out for anyone who would not normally come to this little, out of the way town. I saw that the Sheriff kept a file which he shared with the forest rangers when he had enough proof to assist them in apprehending the culprits. Though he never caught him doing anything specific, Perry seemed to puzzle him just enough to warrant interest. A couple of close-up shots of the truck when Perry wasn't in it, nothing visible except a black bag on the passenger side, truck bed clean with no sign of debris indicating what he had been up to. No animal corpses, no chunks of granite rock often taken and sold to craft shops, no copper wire, or jugs of alcohol, just the black bag that was visible in many pictures usually taken in early daylight from outside the window. But the next page I saw gave me an understanding of the Sheriff's motivation for pulling Perry's photo out of what might have been his suspicious character file. A large black and white picture, creased from much handling was in front of the last written page. Smiling at me from across the years was a likeness of Perry and Sierra sitting together, holding hands in what looked like a studio portrait. A number one occupied space in the upper left corner of the paper with a circle around it. In hindsight, I realized that all the pages were numbered according to his special timeline. I had actually started reading notes from another file with dates from a year earlier. The scraps of paper in the back were written at a later time, not connected with the other material until later. The earlier sheets were different, without lines, as were the numbers on the top. Apparently, Richardson had put them together after seeing the picture; somehow adding the element of the missing women during his search for Sierra. Faded black ink on the back of the photograph proclaimed the couple to be Jimmy and Sierra. According to Sierra's mother, who had written a short letter to go with the picture, Jimmy had left town a year before Sierra had disappeared. Sierra had been crazy about Jimmy, but he was restless, wanting out of town to go to bigger and better places. It was hard for Sierra at first, but when he failed to keep in touch, she seemed to be getting on with her life. *I went through her things*, Sierra's mother wrote, *and couldn't find any correspondence. I haven't heard or seen from Jimmy in quite a while, he had no family to ask and while the local police thought they might be together* she knew in her heart they weren't. Mrs. Glenn went on to express her dismay that her daughter's disappearance was hidden on page seven of the paper while the tragic but explainable car crash of a local grocery store owner occupied the front page. *I'm afraid that she is dead*, this last statement written in pen marks much lighter than the rest of the letter, as if it pained the author to admit this. And then, clipped to the last page was a list and a name, James Durnham. So Sheriff Richardson had known exactly who Perry, I mean James, was the entire time! What was going on here? I guess he really hadn't tried to locate this James because he already knew his identity. Huffing and puffing indignantly, I looked over what he had written about James Durnham. High school athlete, manager of a clothing factory before the economy suffered the full effects of the depression, announced departure after his father died, never seen again. Short, sweet and to the point. But then I noticed he had penciled in a large question mark and two attached articles regarding missing women in the area a few years prior to his leaving town. Three people who knew him casually had mentioned he might have been stepping out on his girl with other women; nothing obvious, but it was a small town and people talked. But, once again, no evidence of murder, no bodies, and he left town not long after. No problems of this kind occurred once he was gone. Enraged, I shook my head, it was all too pat! There really wasn't any concrete evidence to back this all up. I'd never met Adam Richardson but the glimpse I'd had of him, brief as it was, didn't seem stupid or petty. I knew Perry, and still thought of him as Perry. He was scary at times, but I hadn't considered this! Unbidden, my mind went back to Perry's amnesia, being unable to account for most of his life, apart from a few inconsequential and hazy flashes of useless information. Was that the truth or avoidance of things he didn't want to discuss? We were both now in a place where he'd been before, and he hadn't shown any indication that he remembered it. I found that odd but there had to be an explanation for all of this. I was overreacting. My charming friend was only interested in finding himself. Surely he meant no harm to anyone; he'd been so upset when I suggested otherwise. I paused a moment, mentally replaying our conversation. Actually, what he said was, *he didn't remember going back to Jeff.* He wasn't denying it, just telling me he didn't remember, and I had seen nothing to indicate that he had been lying. Yes, he was creepy, but having been dead for so long, he might have been out of practice with the living personality traits he might have once had. I saw them every once in awhile, and I couldn't believe he would hurt anyone intentionally. Jeff, was a killer who'd died of a heart attack, and these women had nothing to do with Perry.

While I sat, pondering this conversation, my eyes were drawn back to the hand-drawn map, seeing it now like I'd seen it for the first time. That's when I noticed a red X in what looked like an area a few miles from the main road into the state park and another mark next to a spot a few miles further down the road. I had studied this map and all its markings a few minutes earlier and swore I had not seen the X or the dark dot implanted inches away from it. Yet here they were, clear as day, drawing my eye to them as if intended. A shifting of the air at my side let me know I was not alone; surprise, surprise. My *dead person's spirit detector* was going off. The residue of a new lifeless energy was seeking me out; it wasn't one of my *regulars,* but, it seemed my circle of followers was expanding. A gray mist shimmered into view on the seat next to me. Every hair on my arm stood at full attention as I turned my head to see a spirit I'd sort of been expecting since I first started reading his notes. Though he presented as gray mist, I knew it was Adam Richardson. I could feel him filling the car with his presence. He wasn't as strong as Perry. I couldn't seem to stop calling him that, but he was determined enough to make me want to cry. I sensed the Sheriff was putting all residual energy into making me aware of him. The file in my hands seemed to take on a life of its own. Papers I'd already read, flew about the car until I was left with holding small slip of thin parchment I'd not seen before, its contents the most revealing of all the things I'd read up to this moment, and I knew I had to go to the spot where Per..., I mean James, had died.

Chapter Thirty-Five-James

Lingering over my dead body in my past reality, I tried to process what this all meant. The Sheriff, I recognized him from his picture in one of the newspaper articles she had been looking at, had driven off with my blood all over the front of his car, after ending my existence on Earth. It didn't appear to have been an accident. Hell, he wasn't even concerned enough to tell anyone I was there. I don't know who found me, but I was, of course, long dead by the time they did. Murdered, left in the middle of the road, and never identified when he "investigated" my case. No wonder he hadn't tried to find out who I was; I was his victim and he didn't want anyone else to know. I didn't even know that man! Why would he kill me? Maddie was seeking answers from a source who had ended my life. I needed to warn her, let her know what had happened. Fueled with righteous anger, I sought a way to escape back to the place where Maddie was, I had to warn her. For all I knew, she was doing exactly what he wanted her to do. Maybe he was the blackness we both had seen. Anyone who could kill a complete stranger had to have a dark soul. I was a good man, I hadn't deserved this. I had to warn Maddie that he might come back to hurt her. I had to help her. Reluctantly leaving my body, I moved back toward the nothing I had come from but couldn't find the way out. It was a cruel twist of fate that I was forced to remain in a memory I didn't want to be a part of. Blank eyes staring out at nothing, me dead, dead, dead. I didn't remember any of this happening all that time ago. I don't remember dying this way! What was this!

Turning to look around me, seeing nothing but trees, I tried to avoid looking at my body as it was then, seeking a way to end this memory or whatever I was trapped in. I had been dead for eighty years and this was my first memory of my final moments. My life had been cut short for no reason and I deserved to know why. Searching a memory that fell woefully short of anything beyond the emerging realization that I was an overachiever from a dysfunctional family, I tried to force the recollections to come. Nothing. I was a good man! I didn't deserve this! How had I even gotten here, a place in the middle of nowhere? I didn't see a car nearby. Had the lawman brought me here and then killed me? It didn't seem possible that we could have had contact and I not remember any of it. I did not know that man, how I got where I was, or why I had to die. It was hellish being trapped in this situation. I had to get out of here! What good was being a lifeless wisp of air if I couldn't even navigate through a dimension that only existed in the past? Continuing to avoid the sight of my body, I sped around the small section of road I seemed confined to, noticing for the first time the shady images lingering on the edges of this reality. Seven in all, the shapes hung in the darkness through which no other image showed, all focused on, it seemed, my dead body. Had they been like a welcoming committee for newly deceased persons? If this is what happened when I died, they certainly hadn't done their job, because I don't recall any of them trying to draw me into the wonderful, adventurous, afterworld to join with them. I had just been sucked in to drift aimlessly for the longest time. I tried to approach one of the forms, but it shrank away from me before I got close. Changing tactics, I swerved to another one, getting the same reaction as, one after one, the light-colored shadows faded into the place where the world ended, and nothing could be seen. Cries of agony sounded in the air from some place distant; memories of what had been heard at some point in my life but not connected with anything I could put my finger on. Pleas for mercy, laughter that held no joy, anger hidden behind a charming smile. The urge to complete a mission, heartbreak, betrayal, the end of a good man. All these things came at me in a rush until all I could think of was to get out of here. I had to find Maddie and finish things. I knew what I had to do. I was suddenly aware of my importance, of an unfinished destiny I needed to continue. With the greatest of relief, I saw a thin area of trees that seemed to go on longer than the location would suggest it should. Racing toward it, I found myself in the nothingness once again, seeking a way back to Maddie. Gray puffiness gave way to opaque white as I re-entered the present world and found the young man emptying trash outside the hotel she'd been staying in. Slipping in with an ease from frequent practice, I concentrated on finding Maddie through our special connection.

Chapter Thirty-Six-Maddie

I drove toward the state park as fast as I could without breaking the law, Sheriff Richardson's agonizing confession playing in my head over and over. As well buried as it had been among all his notes, I was sure I'd been the first person to see it since he'd written it. That, and the fact that he'd retired with a spotless record, never having been convicted of the murder he'd committed. Yes, I'd seen it in black and white, the neatly printed note stating he'd hit Perry with his car and gone home. *When I first started looking into James Durnham*, the Sheriff had continued with his explosive statement. *It was merely because he was out of place. So many visits to that hotel; no one was sure what he was doing here. I thought maybe he was poaching or running some moonshine, it happened out here a lot. I never confronted him, just watched, it's my experience that all men make a mistake eventually if you pretend you don't notice them. Let them settle into their routine and get comfortable, but never let your guard down. His nice blue truck showed up every couple months. Always clean, never with any evidence of carrying any cargo; I checked when he was sleeping. Nothing extra in the truck bed, no trace of heavy objects being hauled around. In fact, it was pristine. Staff reported late nights out, followed by sleeping into the afternoon. Might have been a family guy stepping out for a bit of a wild time, we had seen that a time or two among the wealthier set, but those were hard times, not too many men had money to throw around like that. He was a puzzle, until Harriet Glenn's daughter disappeared, and I realized he had known her. I wouldn't have even gotten involved if my beloved Franny hadn't asked, but once I did I couldn't seem to stop digging into this man's life. According to Sierra's mother, he'd left town a year before she did, but no one was quite sure where he'd gone or what he had been doing since he lost his job. I was the only one who knew he'd been here. I probably wouldn't have gone further because there was no evidence to work with, had it not been for the dreams; dreams like I'd never had before in my life. The visions, as I'd come to call them, since dreams seemed to be a tame description, were so clear and detailed, staying with me for days until I felt compelled to write them down. Each nightly episode had a name and a general location which, to my surprise, when I looked into them, actually existed. I'm a practical man*, Adam Richardson wrote to me from far in the past. It was strange that I truly felt as though he was writing directly to me, telling me everything I needed to know as if aware I would be reading it. That was impossible, but the strange feeling of one on one contact with this man over decades of time past sent shivers down my spine. I don't know why I would think this since I was well aware of the strange things that could happen in this world. I'd had months of spooky and downright terrifying experiences with the existence of things beyond the norm. Sheriff Richardson went on to say that he knew the women were dead, they told him so. He couldn't prove it, didn't have bodies to show anyone, no evidence to share with his fellow lawmen. Who would believe a man who said dead women spoke to him?

Actually, it was more than just dead Sierra. She seemed to be the loudest voice, getting his attention until he couldn't deny the truth. Sierra visited him every night, bringing the other women with her, showing him their tragedies until he was distressingly familiar with them all. He had researched and written down all he had learned about the last days of their lives. For a while that was okay. It seemed to make Sierra happy, or so Sheriff Richardson thought. He wrote about a short time of wonderful, dreamless sleep, but once it became apparent that he could go no further with his investigation due to lack of solid evidence, she returned with a vengeance. He woke up one night from the worst nightmares he ever had to find a dark form hovering by his bed; the rest of the night was a blur.

I remember the feeling of urgency to get something done, he wrote, *knew he was close by, had come back to hide her body. She was in me and so everything I felt was her. She had been dead for months and that bastard had returned to sit by her grave. Well, she wasn't at rest, she was angry. He had to answer for what he did. I couldn't stop myself from getting in my car and going where she directed me; my eyes told me I was in the state park, but I wasn't in control of what I did. It was pitch black, I couldn't break free and he was just there, running across the road. My foot hit the gas pedal, somewhere outside my head, I heard the thump and knew he wouldn't be alive when I got out to look at his body. I had exacted revenge, driven off, and not looked back, leaving his body to be found by someone else as I cleaned up all evidence of my having been there. I had done what Sierra wanted, but hadn't been me when I did it. Justice had been served but I couldn't tell anyone when there was no proof. Sierra had left me, taking her knowledge and personal issues with her, and I was left to live with the vague memory of what I had done. I write this now, a useless confession. I will never tell anyone about this, but will have to live with it nonetheless. I wasn't me, he asserted again. I was an instrument. She was done with me. I played my part. But it's not over. This is the only certainty I have left from this nightmare; something is still undone. I searched for years and didn't find the women I knew to be dead. He died and I let him rot in anonymity but couldn't shake the feeling that Sierra was far from finished with James. He never had to answer for anything he did. As loathe as I am to admit it. I did the right thing, I'm sure I saved lives, and someday, someone will find what I could not.*

Glancing down at the cardboard folder housing this startling document, the official seal of the Sheriff's office stamped on top, I got the impression the Sheriff might have intended to bring it to the office but for some reason it lay simmering on his desk at home, waiting to boil over. The last sentence was the only indication he hadn't written it just to clear his conscience. If not, he surely had changed his mind or it would have been seen long before I came along. How could he have known about me? That was just ridiculous. I mean, he wasn't a psychic or anything, just a smart guy who'd been possessed once in his life, telling me, from beyond the grave somehow, that Perry was a serial killer who he'd run over with his car while under the influence of some dead woman. What kind of bad movie plot was this! Perry was a nice guy, it had to be a mistake. Other than several trips to this area on what could have been business, he had nothing to tie my ghost guy to any women. It was all just dreams, guessing, and the influence of some dead woman who didn't exactly say it was Perry who killed her. She just said she was killed. If Perry had done it, wouldn't the Sheriff have found Sierra's body somewhere close to where he had run over my friend? This could all have been one big mistake. I didn't understand half of what my ghost visitors had been trying to tell me. He may have known Sierra but that didn't mean he had killed her. All his evidence said Perry/James had left town long before she disappeared. I would have known if Perry were an evil killer. I would have sensed it.

All these thoughts ran through my head as I drove instinctively to the place it had all happened. I eased up onto the side of the road, heart in my throat as the internal argument raged on. I hadn't needed a map. The pictures hadn't distinguished this spot from any others in this wooded area, but I knew without a doubt that I was standing in the spot where James Durnham had taken his last breath. His body had been decomposing in a John Doe's grave for eighty years, the blood from this crime had long since been washed away with many rainfalls, but in my mind a large black X marked the spot. I stood, looking at the bare stretch of concrete I'd been led to, wondering why my presence was required here. A faint tingling in the air reminded me that I was never alone for long. Turning toward the source of my newly arrived companion, I was not so startled to find the darkness hovering near the trees behind me. I was, however, not prepared for what happened next. In a move I failed to anticipate, she rushed toward me, diving into my body like a swimmer into deep water. Sierra Glenn took control, burrowing in, and refusing to move no matter how hard I tried to push her out. As I screamed obscenities at my intruder, ordering her to leave, she stayed put, both of us waiting for someone we were sure would soon join us.

Chapter Thirty-Seven-James

I'd lucked out. He had enough sense to lead me to his car before I took over completely. It was a ratty little modern number with many dents which, much to my surprise, started immediately after I turned the key. Rattling and chugging in our dilapidated chariot, my unwilling transporter began driving me where I needed to go. At this point, I knew exactly where I was heading, guided by remerging memories and a hunger to visit places long neglected. I had so much to tell Maddie; I was Jimmy, a well-liked, respected young man who'd died in the 1930's after a Sheriff hit him with a police car and drove away. I was an innocent victim who happened to be in the wrong place at the wrong time. I was a good guy; I'd seen enough to know I was a good guy. I knew right from wrong, the world knew me as a really, good man. My hobbies were justified. Those girls I liked to visit were just like the ones my father would sleep with behind my mother's back. She knew about them but never said anything. I knew too. I saw how much it hurt her, made her drink so much it rotted out her liver. She died just after I graduated high school. And Dad, well, he had an accident a year later and left me too. That loss was less traumatic. But I always had Sierra, from grammar school on. It was always understood that we would marry. I adored her, and she felt the same. Then it all changed one day, things got rough, the factory I had been managing closed; it was happening all over the country. I found myself with a lot of time on my hands and a growing anger toward the world around me. A popular, well-educated man such as myself forced to find odd jobs to earn money. At first, it was alright because I had the house my father left me. But after a time of not being able to find much to do in the area, I became increasingly frustrated. That's when my hobby started. The women relieved the stress and made me feel less like a loser, unable to support the woman he loved. No money equaled no marriage. It was an understood fact at the time. So, here I was, Sierra so close and yet still so far away, and those women were just all around me, a reminder of all the bad things that had happened in my life. I would have had a happy home life if it hadn't been for women like that. If not for them, my father would have been faithful, my mother would have been a satisfied housewife without a drinking problem, and maybe even have survived to love much longer than she had. Now I, the smart man, the popular man, the good man, was reduced to menial labor to eat, while the love of my life worked six days a week and brought home more money than I did. I could see the way her parents looked at me. They had known me all their lives and now I wasn't good enough for Sierra. The women, what I did with them made me feel more like a man, and it helped for a while, but it changed me too. Sierra noticed. She started to ask questions. She sensed I was hiding something, but I couldn't tell her about the women, so I pretended everything was the same. We went on as we always had for a little longer, but I became a little more restless and angry and she, a little more distant. I felt I needed to do something different, I wanted her just as much, but had to prove myself. I had to get enough money to marry my perfect girl. Our relationship was strained and we agreed to part for a time. I tried not to think about how she seemed relieved when I said that, but I couldn't help myself; the thought festered in my mind as I left town. Rather than cooling off while I was gone, it seemed I got angrier. I had more time to think. I missed her like crazy but couldn't go back until my situation improved and *they* were always around, stirring up all kinds of emotions I didn't want to feel. Once again, women were part of my problem yet I sought them out when I was away from her. I had my fun and left them to return to a regular life.

More odd jobs and months of traveling around always to come back to the same area to unburden myself of all I had done. The woods were a peaceful place to lose myself, to hide all the sins I'd committed. I always told myself, all it would take were a few more and I could go back to Sierra; clean and ready to take care of her. I'd saved a little money from doing things that may have been outside the law, but desperate times called for desperate measures. I was clever, keeping to the shadows, never using my real name, making sure none of this would follow me on my path back to respectability. Some thefts, dealings with illegal alcohol transport, never in my own truck, always theirs, stepping just over the line of what was allowed by the law. But throughout it all I was still a good man. My motives were pure; I could leave all this behind as soon as I accomplished what I needed to. I was a good man.

My life was becoming clearer by the second. It all made sense as I came to remember who I was. Playing out as it was, I failed to understand why it took me so long to recall these things which didn't seem so bad when reasoned out. Maybe it was my sudden and traumatic death.

146

I had so much to tell Maddie. She had to know she could stop looking now. All her information would have come from my murderer anyway. I knew what happened. I could tell her to stop looking into this. I was a good man who had just wanted to go back to the true love of his life. I was dead and I'm sure after all this time, so was she, but maybe the memories were enough to help me find her in the afterworld. Maybe we could be together again, all the time spent apart would melt away and she would look at me the way she had when we walked the halls of the high school holding hands, kissing passionately in dark places, talking about our future with lots of children. As I drove down the now familiar road, I shook my borrowed head, trying to rid my mind of visions of my beautiful Sierra screaming, running in a scene I was sure couldn't have happened because I loved her and would protect her at all costs. I was close now, just a turn or two away and this would all be resolved. Maddie would stop looking for answers in the wrong place and help me find Sierra. It was time we both got peace.

Chapter Thirty-Eight-Maddie

We waited, Sierra and I, feeling him coming closer. I felt her emotions, her resolve to confront him. I tried to evict her but, passing on her regrets, she stayed put and, in my body, stood at the side of the road in the dimming light of day, certain we would soon see him again. I shared her sorrow and rage as they coursed through my form. It was very quiet here, the only sound we heard was the chirping symphony of crickets. I breathed, she breathed with me, anticipation making my heart flutter at this long-awaited reunion. In this very short, serene moment, I thought how odd it would be to explain this to anyone, should I even be foolish enough to try. She was strong enough to climb onboard, but I was there enough to know what was going on and prevent her from taking over entirely. Knowing what she had made Sheriff Richardson do all those years ago when I was pretty sure she hadn't been dead all that long, told me her purpose was fueled by the strongest of emotions. But equally as desperate to not involuntarily murder anyone, I pushed back hard enough to get her attention. I could evict her alright, but it was going to be a hell of a fight and she seemed to want my cooperation; this was a significant moment for her. So I stayed put, stubbornly refusing to let her have me entirely. In turn she shared the knowledge that this was between the two of them only. Which was ridiculous, really. How was that supposed to work out since he was a ghost and we were, essentially a live person, namely me. Why couldn't they just work this out amongst themselves? I mean, it wasn't like they hadn't both been dead for quite some time. Didn't the afterworld have some kind of reunion thing? Why did they have to drag me into it? Then I heard the rattle and chug of a car that should be put out of its misery and understood why she chose to find a body, to face the one he was bringing. Yes, at this point, I was aware of what was about to happen as the vehicle drew to a stop a few feet away; a tall man with long hair stepped out of it. The kid had to have been in his late-teens, not much younger than myself, though due to current circumstances, I felt at least a century older. Poor kid had that blank, panicked look on his face that Frank, the killer mailman, had worn as he walked, step by reluctant step toward me. But I guess Perry had been practicing a bit because that look was soon gone, to be replaced by one of recognition at seeing me. Sierra pulled back a bit and let me talk. I guess she didn't want Per…, I mean James (this crap was so confusing!) to know she was here yet.

"Maddie," he said. This guy had a very deep southern accent and every word came through much clearer than when James's spirit spoke to me. "I know everything now! You can stop looking for answers from the cop's records." A brief pause, lips turned down, possessed guy pointed to the road in front of me. "That bastard hit me with his car. I died right there but I don't know why he did it." Each word spit from his lips in restrained rage while he told his version of events. A justified man venting his rage at a life cut short.

"So you now know who you are?" My lips spoke the words, but she was listening, waiting for an opportunity to speak.

"Yes, my name is James Durnham, I was a good man killed by that Sheriff. I remember it all now. I was crossing the road, he sped up, hit me, got out and looked, then drove away after seeing I was dead."

"Why would he do that?" she injected just enough shock into my voice to show him that living Maddie was listening and reacting the way he expected. Adding for effect, "And who is this boy?" Waving my hand up and down in front of his new personal puppet.

"I found him by the hotel," his voice answered quietly, now that his original outburst had ended, and he realized he had to find a logical explanation for using this young man to find me. "I got excited about what I found and had to keep you safe from that murder. I think he is that black cloud we saw moving around in *there*. You know, the dead place. He's dangerous. I wasn't strong enough to find you without some help. I used all my energy to get back from the other side. I knew you'd wind up here eventually; smart girl that you are, it was inevitable." It seemed like that compliment was added for affect. "I had to let you know I was a good man. You don't need to know anything else," the boy finished with a deep breath.

We listened, neither of us believing his reasoning. I wondered why she wasn't saying anything, still letting him believe he was talking to just Maddie. What were we waiting for? Extra company or not, I was about to get aggressive and kick her to the curb, but must admit, the longer he talked, my curiosity got the better of me. I guess a little part of me wanted him to tell me he'd remembered something like his innocence, for all Sierra and the Sheriff thought they'd known to be wrong. She never actually showed him killing her, it was all just circumstantial evidence, right? They were guessing. I flinched as she shared her last living vision, James's face looking down at her. He was crying as his hands closed around her throat, squeezing, and bringing them face to face in an oddly intimate moment in which she stopped breathing and he kissed her lips. She hovered above their forms seconds later watching him cry and cover her face so he wouldn't have to look at her anymore.

"Talking her out of looking any further; you always were such a charmer Jimmy," this the first indication that it wasn't me speaking.

"Just like the first time we met in the fifth grade, when you knocked down that bully who stole my lunch money. My hero, the handsome boy who carried my books to class and kissed me behind the library when we were thirteen. All that fumbling around in the garden shed, never quite going all the way. Wait until we're married, you said, but that didn't happen, did it?" My companion pushed me as far back as I would allow and still be not entirely her. Her personality showed through, letting itself be known to him. She wanted me to hear. It never was about hurting or frightening me. It was about rage, betrayal, and the need to make him admit what he had done.

"Sierra?" The young man looked at me disbelievingly. We must've looked an odd pair, me and the teenager, talking like old friends, or lovers.

"Where have you been?" He walked closer while we backed up, not wanting contact with either of them. "I have been so lost. The only thing I could remember was you. I think we argued, and you left me," James spoke in his new body. "What happened to you? I think I was looking for you when I was run down by that lawman." This was said in an accusatory tone, as though his death was related to her abandonment.

"You had just visited the place you buried me when you were run down by the lawman," Sierra spat out with what I thought was an enormous amount of control considering what I now knew to be true.

There was a long silence followed by a sharp intake of breath; her announcement had the intended effect. His vessel's face blanched in shock.

"What!" He shook his head vigorously. "I loved you; I wasn't perfect, but I loved you! I would never have hurt you. I was a good man. You must be confused." Smiling, like I was to be pitied, James reached his hands out to me. Despite the anger and fear, her heart reacted like it must have so many times in the past when she wanted to believe his lies. Long, unexplained absences, how odd he acted when he came back. She had been so much in love, but over time, things had changed to the point that she felt a sense of relief when he had to leave town to look for a job. How could you love someone and be glad they were leaving you? And when he returned, all charming, almost like he was when they were in school together; apologetic, asking for a chance to explain she had listened, wanting to believe him. The ride that took her further than she thought they were going; growing unease; the nightmare ending to her life, these memories overrode her flash of sentimentality, and were replaced by the anger she had carried around for over eighty years.

"Were the other women confused too?" We stood there, all four of us, in that secluded place having a confrontation that was long overdue.

"Other women?" He gave a small laugh, followed by a puzzled look. "Surely after all these years you can't be angry over a few indiscretions!" My lips curled in disgust, not because I told them to; it was still all her. "Indiscretions? Is that what you think they were?"

"I was weak. Those women were not what you were. Sierra, you were the one true thing in my life. They were dirty and didn't need to be here anymore."

The hair rose up on my arms as he spoke with conviction, without giving it any thought, as if being honest for a second before gathering himself together and repeating his mantra. "I was a good man." There was a slight pause, then a puzzled look came over his borrowed face before he changed the tone of the conversation. I think we wandered into an area he did not like. "I came back for you. I left for a whole year to get things out of my system, but I came back for you." Bit by bit, new information came out, always skirting around the little bombshell she'd dropped about her own demise and his other victims; back to things James had begun to recall.

"You should have known I would have come back for you. All that time apart only made me want you more. I had no job, no hope of taking care of you once we married, I had to get my act together. Those impulses I had, well, they were all part of working it out. Men have to get experience somewhere before we settle for a family. They weren't missed and when it was over, I was alright. I felt better. I even made some money from a few things. No real job, but I couldn't stay away. I was a good man, anything that happened was not my fault, just a little fun and I was coming back to you." All explanations came back to the same thing: I was a good man.

"You killed all those women," Sierra said slowly, letting each word hang in the air between them, waiting for him to acknowledge what he had done.

"No, darling, they placed themselves in danger. I'm a good man. I'm sure they were just fine when I left them; they were where they belonged. They served their purpose and I didn't need them anymore."

This odd conversation was getting odder by the minute, wavering between almost admission, to reasons why it couldn't be true. It was beginning to dawn on me that James had blocked out anything negative from his life. Part of the story was held back, parts I'm pretty damn sure I needed to know.

"Where did you leave them?" Sierra pushed him to speak but he was silent, lips clamped together, shifting from foot to foot in an odd kind of shuffle.

"I'm not sure what you're talking about," his reply was long in coming and so low as to barely be heard. A lengthy pause, in which he seemed to be thinking, "I parked my truck somewhere nearby. I wonder why they never found it?" All this said as if he hadn't just been accused of killing Sierra and several other women. "I don't remember ever hurting you. I was always so good to you, you know that. Maybe the Sheriff killed you too." Words spilled out of his mouth in a rush of incomprehensible logic, hope that this was true made him smile and his eyes widen in the oddest way. Sierra and I listened in disbelief as he approached another step or two, a look of desperation on his face, gesturing behind him. "Please, Sierra, I can show you. You have to understand. I was a good man."

Then, having said what he needed to say, James turned and walked toward the woods with a wave of his hand, indicating we should follow. And we did, not because I wanted to, but because Sierra made me; this was her moment and she wasn't going to give up until he had faced up to what he had done.

Chapter Thirty-Nine-James

Sierra was here. It took her long enough to get through, but I should have known she loved me enough to find her way back to me. Shame she was so confused. Then again, I had been too when I first returned. Bits and pieces of my life were falling into place now; I was sure it would all be set right soon. I had come back for her all those years ago; I knew that now. But all that other nonsense just couldn't be true. There was no way I could have killed her. I had turned to them because of her, for her protection. Those dirty women had been my version of sexual education. They meant nothing to me. I used them just like my father had, but wasn't about to make the same mistakes. No one would have any idea what I was doing, especially the woman I loved. I hid my hobby well. I was a good man; I would get it all out of the way before I married Sierra, doing what I wanted, but giving none of them a chance to take it any further. They were my secret, a secret I intended to keep. What we did was fantasy. I let all my urges come to the surface and left them in a place where they couldn't intrude on reality. I was a good man, a handsome catch. It wouldn't do to have any of them seeking me out to be more than just a one-night stand. They could never tell. I left them far from my world so they could never invade it. Sierra must never know what I did. I searched outside of town, leaving her when I felt overwhelmed by needs she wouldn't understand. Then I lost my job, my dignity and it got worse. I needed my outlet even more, to the point where it physically hurt not to go *hunting*. That was a strange way to put it, but hunting seemed the only apt term to describe what I was doing. After all, it meant to seek something, and I was indeed looking for a particular-something, a kind of release.

It was a rough time for me. I was so far from having the woman I adored, was no longer the hero of the high school playing field, days as boss to those less educated and talented than me were over, and I was left humbled and angry.

Memories of our history began to come at me faster, filling in blank spots that had existed for what seemed like forever. Sierra had been such a big part of my life; the one constant in a world where I felt I had to appear good enough while secretly believing I wasn't. Growing up with parents I had begun to despise as I learned more about them and their weaknesses, was tolerable only because of her. She had been at my side the entire miserable time, giving comfort and support when I needed it the most, standing at my side when first one, then the other of my pitiful sires thankfully took their last breaths, freeing me from the pretense of loving them. She was all I could think about, the perfect woman. With most people I'd had to blend, pretending to experience emotions I don't think I'd ever had, but not with Sierra. With her I felt, I mean actually *felt* something, like what I imagined others might feel for a fellow human being. Lust and anger came naturally to me, but kinder things were just an afterthought mentioned in books, emotions I'd had to act out for others to be accepted as one of them.

And I had fit in just fine for the longest time, all because of her; working and interacting like someone who cared about other people. When the factory closed, I didn't have my day to day distractions; behaving like others had become more difficult and I think she saw that. That was understandable after all I had been through, she should have been patient enough to wait it out. I would have gotten control again, but Sierra began to pull away. I could sense it in the way she would sometimes look at me. She seemed afraid. I would never hurt her, but our petting sessions only served to make me want more, and at that time I couldn't risk getting her pregnant; couldn't afford to support a wife and child. I might have gotten a little rough at times but managed to stop myself before anything happened. I'll admit that I was frustrated with her, too. I mean, she was working more than I was. Couldn't she tell that I was supposed to take care of her? It was demeaning. I tried not to act offended when she offered to get me a job at the grocery store. She meant well, but I was better than that. I couldn't be seen working alongside people I graduated with and secretly knew I was better than. No, that would never do. The itch to do something important got stronger and stronger, leaving me with the need to escape and scratch it. I had begun to realize that maybe what I was doing went beyond calming myself down. I was contributing to society in a way that few could. I was making the world clean for men like me, good men. Because no matter what else happened, it was always important for everyone to know I was a good man.

As my sneakered feet moved over the overgrown path, I never once hesitated. It was as if I had been here many times before. I had a flash of navigating the terrain in the fading light with little difficulty. The sound of snapping twigs and rustling branches told me Maddie's occupied body was doing as I requested, following me where I wanted her to. Sierra always had a difficult time resisting me when I poured on the charm. It would all soon be like it had been before. There might be a few things I'd change this time, but we would always be together.

Slipping once again into deep thought, I allowed my mind to travel to times past. What was it I was trying to recall? I had come back for Sierra, unable to stay away from her any longer. Sitting in my car in late afternoon, aware that she would be returning from work any time now, I waited with my heart in my throat, going over exactly what I would say to her before sweeping her off her feet again. At first, she might be a bit angry, I reasoned. A year was a long time to be away with no word, but Sierra would welcome me back with open arms. She was my girl. I sat for what seemed like forever, rehearsing my speech, the one I knew would win her over like so many times in the past; expecting to see her walking down the sidewalk toward her parent's house any second. To my surprise she did indeed arrive there, but it was in a sleek green sedan driven by Foster Hurst, the owner of the store she worked in. I watched him get out, walk around to her side of the car and escort her to the front door before planting a kiss on her lips in a very unboss-like manner. I was pleased to see her pull away and quickly walk inside, but not quite sure whether it was for some other reason than the kiss. How long had this been developing? Foster had been a classmate in high school, he knew she was mine!

My memories were not doing me any favors now, because the pain at seeing this was so intense it was causing my current body to stop and double over like I'd been kicked in the stomach. Gulping in air, I scowled at my companion, seeing Maddie but knowing it was Sierra. She hadn't waited for me! She should have known I would be back. But she had replaced me with another man. It had taken a huge amount of restraint not to go over and punch him repeatedly in the face, but that would only serve to let others know I was here. This new situation changed my plans. What I had in mind this time required as much stealth as I had employed with other ventures, and so stilled my hand from any emotional outbursts I might have been inclined to commit.

That night, I had waited, recollections suddenly spilling into my head like water bursting from a dam. The pain and need for vengeance was as fresh as it had been all that time ago.

He left, and I went to the side of her house, entering through her bedroom window on the first floor as I had in the past. Those times we just talked for hours, sitting by the creek close to her house, talking about our dreams for the future. This time I was different, I needed to win her back. She had always been looked at longingly by other boys, the only thing keeping her safe was the fact that she was my girl. Those boys wouldn't have dared to make a move on my beautiful Sierra as long as I was around. I took a deep breath and tried to understand her vulnerability in my absence. After all, she was a helpless female without her man to protect her. I could forgive her but certainly not him. I'd have to make sure he knew I was not pleased with his behavior. That would have to wait until we made up and she was under my protection again. I had to let her know it was alright, I was back. She looked so surprised when I greeted her as she walked through the door. At first a little angry, then allowing me to hug her.

"You've been gone a long time," were her first words, her embrace a bit stiff and awkward. I could tell she was wondering how long I'd been here. Had I seen the kiss? I always could read her like a book. I was apologetic and understanding. Bringing up our past at every possible opportunity, until she smiled and relaxed. I told her a few white lies. I had a job, I'd said, working hard. I'd managed to save some money and hoped to reignite our old flame.

But she had to be honest. "I've been seeing someone," she said. "It hasn't been long. I haven't even told Mom and Dad yet, but he's been good to me and I like him very much. He was very comforting when you left and never contacted me." Though said softly, I caught the note of accusation in her voice.

Why did she have to be like that? She had to be made to understand, it had all been for her.

If the past had taught me anything, it was that I should never show her when I was angry, that's not what good men did. My anger was for those harlots only. I tried not to dwell on the fact that I enjoyed their fear. I was a good man. So, I just smiled and told her I understood but would she just humor me and go out for coffee and talk for a while? If this was to be the end for us, I just wanted a chance to explain and show her what I'd been doing while I was away. My charming smile won her over. As it was still early, she had time to visit with me before her parents arrived, then maybe I could stay for dinner. That would be lovely, I'd told her. Secure in the way things had gone, she gathered her things and walked with me to my car.

A few steps more-another flash-me driving. I was just going to find a spot and talk to her. That was my first intention. But the longer we were in the car, the stronger my urge became to make her see the error of her ways. I continued past the place we should have stopped, watching her surprised look when we passed first the town sign and then the state marker. I listened with half an ear to her demands to know where I was taking her and that I stop and drive her back home. Acting like the adult in the car, I insisted she stop talking for a while and give me a moment to find a place to talk. We made it to the woods. Sitting in the car, I tried to reason with her, to explain that I just needed her to understand all the sacrifices I'd made while we were apart. The odd jobs, staying away from her, how betrayed I felt when I came back to find her kissing another man. She just sat there, as far to the side of the cab as she could, listening to me pour my heart out with that *look* on her face. I don't know why, even though she didn't speak, she was making me furious. I missed her smile, the way she was always touching my arm, hung on every word I said. Then I remembered how she always said that honesty was important to her, how she could forgive anything for love if there were nothing but truth between us. She had said that during one of our late-night talks after she had heard rumors about me and that cheesy blonde girl from school. I hadn't told the truth back then; I was just an irresponsible teenager, but it was never too late to change. I took a deep breath and told her I understood about her and Foster because I had seen a few women while I was away. I didn't want to anger her, but knew it had always been an unspoken worry of hers that I might stray. I told her they meant nothing, and it would stop if she just came to her senses and reunited with me. We were meant to be together. In my eagerness to get her to understand, I reached under the seat of my car and pulled out a small black bag. Speaking soothingly, like the good man who'd always made the decisions for us, I assured her I was willing to settle down and give her everything we'd always talked about. She responded by telling me, a year was a long time; she'd changed, she'd realized that things were not as wonderful as I remembered them, and that she needed to move on. Her lips trembled as she asked me to take her home.

I continued talking almost as if she hadn't said anything at all, bringing up all our shared experiences throughout school, how much she'd meant to me; how she had been different from all the other girls, and that I'd always love her. It was during this time I'd begun to talk about her in the past tense, my jaw getting tighter. She began to seem like all those other women I'd left behind me; it was getting harder to maintain control. How could I have been so wrong?

My facial expression must have given away what I was holding back, because she couldn't move far enough toward the door. Here we were, in the middle of nowhere, me trying to deal with a broken heart and she suddenly wanting to be as far from me as possible.

Because I was a good man, I gave her one more chance. Perhaps I'd gone about this all wrong. Things were getting out of hand. You don't give up on someone you love that easy. Composing my face, I tried to defuse the situation by convincing her I was serious. Opening the bag, I laid out my case for her. These women were not what you are; little hard paper cards with names, addresses, hair color, eye color, not showing what they really were, expendable. I told her that she was my everything and I could no longer live without her. Holding the identities of my infidelities in her hands, Sierra fell very quiet, and I was overcome by the depth of my feelings for her, looking in disbelief at the defining characteristics of women who weren't as good as her. Emboldened, I pressed harder to convince her it was okay. We were together, and I wasn't going anywhere again. Leaning closer, breathing in the scent of her perfume, I sought the familiar softness of her lips, taking her silence as an invitation. After all, I was a good man, she knew that. My affectionate advances were cut short by a yelp of surprise as sharp fingernails scraped down my face. To my horror, I lashed out at my beloved Sierra, knocking her head against the passenger window, smearing blood on the clear glass.

Screaming a denial, I walked faster, hoping to dispel this vision. I saw a familiar shape faintly outlined against the fading light and walked toward my truck, still there after all this time. Breathing a relieved sigh, I reached for the plants in front of me, I was sure I would find something in there to show me I'd remembered it all wrong. I was a good man; I just knew it.

Chapter Forty-Maddie

Tall kid came to a stop in front of an overgrowth of brush which, upon closer inspection, proved to be a vehicle. "Still parking here?" Sierra's voice came from my lips. "I remember; this is where you took me the last night of my life, where you tried to convince me you still loved me, just before you killed me. Isn't it a romantic spot?" She mocked as we watched him move toward the clump of plants; pulling vines and brush away from metal, long rusted from exposure to the elements. It had been here this entire time, hidden from view, though I seriously doubted anyone had looked for it. Most of the foliage was loose and was easily removed, seeming to have been simply placed on top to intentionally camouflage it from the casual passerby.

"We struggled and you hit your head," was his short reply. "I didn't intend to hurt you. You attacked me," he said, as tears fell from the young man's eyes, while James used him to express his own emotions.

"I fought back Jimmy." Sierra showed me more as she walked behind his vessel, carefully keeping our distance from him. "You brought me here to clear your conscience and show me your trophies."

"Trophies?" A small snicker filled the air, sending an impression of disdain across the distance while he pulled at the metal door. It creaked and groaned in protest at the lack of function of the long unused hinges. I got the feeling that I was getting a glimpse of some of the things Sierra had noticed from time to time throughout their relationship. He was always so careful to be pleasing and charming, but, every once in a while, she would look into his eyes and see something primitive and mocking there. He would say mean things which he would explain away as a misunderstanding, or he would get rough with her when she would have allowed him to go further with the kissing and groping sessions they participated in. At these times, his lips would curl up, looking a bit disgusted at her willingness to let him touch her intimately before pushing her away. The times when he was scary, she now knew, were truer to who he really was than any other time she'd known him.

"I showed you pieces of paper, things I'd taken from them," all calm and reasonable, like talking to a silly child.

"No, Jimmy," Sierra said, using me to face him, "You showed me fingers."

163

The boy began to shake his head, forcing the door open further. Crinkling of leather spilled out into the night while his lanky body crawled onto the truck's faded and torn leather, reaching onto the seat for the black bag, still sitting upon it. Weathered and cracked from partial exposure to the elements, its contents hidden since James had last closed it and gone out into the road, never to return.

"What the hell are you talking about? I'm a good man! All I kept of theirs were identification cards. I had to prove to you, I sent them away; they weren't good women. I couldn't have you find out about them, so I sent them away and took all evidence of their existence." Words spilled out of the host's lips at a faster pace as James pulled the bag closer to him. The rusted metal clasp protested, finally snapping open after a few curse-filled attempts. He then thrust the bag in my direction without studying its contents. I guess he was so certain what Sierra would see, and felt the need to prove she was wrong. Nubby little objects fell out, tumbling on the ripped material of the seat and down onto the floorboard, followed by the paper cards he had so proudly confessed to taking. I was standing close enough to the door, with just enough sunshine present, to see several pale gray lumps, with chalky nubs sticking out of the end of them, scattered in the small cab. One or two still had garish red or pink polish present on the fingernails. I was astonished to find my lips curling up in a smug smile as the truth of her words became known, followed by a cry of surprise from James when he saw what had landed on the seat.

"No! I was a good man," he said, groping at the digits littering the seat. He seemed to be thinking, trying to find a way to explain their presence in a bag he knew to be his. It took a few minutes of strained silence in which the air around me became cold; I was present enough to feel it. My body shivered, watching my crowded companion go through the contents of his keepsake box, the reality of his past hitting him hard. Whatever was going on inside James's captured brain was making me very uncomfortable. His body movements resembled a puppet being jerked around by its strings. At first, he just started shaking his head in a negative manner as if that alone would make all he was seeing just go away. But the longer he continued to look down at the seat, his face hidden from me, the more pronounced his movements became. Originally, he had been slumped over, closely examining the contents of his little black bag, then suddenly sat straight up, head whipping around to look at me. In turn, I looked back from a great distance, seeing him as an interested viewer might watch a movie with no control over my own movements and conversational skills.

Even as distanced as I was from it all, I was scared. A switch had been flipped and I saw a version of James I suspected had been lurking beneath the surface his entire life, one he'd never shown in civilized company. His demeanor cool and calculated, he tried to continue the conversation as charming James, but it wasn't going well. She already knew who he really was. He was about to say something he never wanted to admit to. But given the evidence laying in the seat behind him, he was unable to do anything but explain it as best he could.

"Those women didn't matter." His tone was tense, each word coming out as if pulled unwillingly from his lips. "They were a necessary weakness; something to keep me civilized." He gave a heavy sigh. "I had urges I couldn't control, urges I had to protect you from. I thought it would be safer to stay away, but I missed you. I had to come back for you." The further he got into his explanation without Sierra moving my body away from him, the lighter his tone became. He relaxed into his excuses with practiced ease. "What happened our last night together was an accident. You overreacted. We struggled. You managed to hit me in the head with something and get out of the car. You were alive then." The conversation stopped abruptly after this confession, as if saying anything else was going too far. We were still not directly discussing what actually happened the last evening of Sierra's life.

"Yes. I was alive. Until you caught up with me and choked me to death," Sierra said each word slowly, as if she wanted no misunderstanding in what she said.

"No!" The shock of her statement made him waver. I could see the boy's body tremble; James was losing control. His legs sagged and back slumped into rusted truck metal causing the door to close with a dull thud. Brown eyes blinked, followed by a panicked, "Where am I?" I could see the boy was awake, free from James's influence, and scared to death. I wanted to reach out to him, but Sierra still had enough of a hold to keep me in the background. We saw James shimmer into view next to his unknown victim, looking both shocked and angry before gathering himself together and slipping back into his flesh suit. The change was immediate and traumatic, shocked expression giving way to rage.

"I was a good man! Your death was your own fault!" As we stood facing each other, the poor boy and I, one possessed person to another. James's anger was releasing a little more information each time.

"My own fault!" she shouted in my voice.

"Yes, you should have listened to me and it would have been alright," he said, his hand reaching toward me. He was close - approaching ever closer - I was not happy with this. I didn't like how this situation was shaping up. I had to do something. Sierra could not just stand there and let this happen. Another few steps and he would be on me, and that's when I saw her reach into my pocket. I don't know when she'd slipped the knife in my pocket, but I felt the wooden hilt against my sensitive fingertips. This had gone too far. She was not going to get her revenge by killing James in another man's body. Clearly, she had lost common sense. Her next statement confirmed my theory.

"Do you know why the Sheriff ran you over?"

"He was crazy? Maybe he wanted to stop me from finishing my work," he suggested. I could see that his mind was working furiously to come up with a logical reason for how he met his end. Her biting tone, the way her eyes gleamed as she looked at him, like she wanted to tell him something badly, caught his attention. He stopped walking and raised his head to look at her expectantly.

"You had killed me months before and buried me with the others," she said. "For some strange reason you kept coming back to tell me how sorry you were. You had just delivered another girl and laid her in my grave. It was dark; bet you didn't know even then, I had the will to stay around my bloated corpse. I hung around, sticking as close to it as I could. It wasn't easy, that light kept trying to call me in. If I had followed it, I wouldn't have been able to take over the Sheriff and make sure he hit you on the way back across from your little burial ground."

There was a strange grunting noise coming from the vicinity of tall guy's mouth as he moved toward my body. I knew what he had in mind. All bets were off. He was furious. She had gone from predictable Sierra, to ungrateful bitch who was responsible for his death. All I could think of was, "oh hell no." I pushed as hard as I could, forcing her to drop the knife and leave my body as I dived to the side to avoid James's attack on me. Ducking behind the rusty vehicle, moving just in time to hear him hit the metal with a thud, I crawled beneath the foliage, putting some distance between us. Burrowing into a thorny hedge, I ignored the scratches and jabs, and put myself so far among the sharp plant life as to make it difficult to follow or pull me out easily. This next part sounds crazy, but I did what instinct told me to and left my body there. I guess desperation drove me to do the one thing I had only been able to do a few times before: spirit travel. I wasn't a master ninja warrior person, just someone who wanted to save myself and the poor helpless boy who was going to be used to kill me.

From high above him, I could hear the curses he was shouting at Sierra, who was also in the vicinity trying to recover from her unexpected expulsion. Her shady form finally manifesting as something resembling her former self, the beautiful dark-haired woman I'd seen in the paper. Occupying space inches from the ground and very close to James and his hapless victim, Sierra lost interest in me for a moment and concentrated her efforts on the young man quickly closing the distance between us. He stumbled around the car and closer to my hiding-place, calling out her name. She followed, getting close enough to whisper in his ear. Stunned, my possessed pursuer stopped and turned to face what she had once been.

"Why?" he asked, with hands up in a pleading gesture.

"I wasn't ready to die; you had no right to take my life," she said, shimmering in and out like a malfunctioning light bulb. "So I took yours." She let out a sharp laugh. "You never would have been caught. You'd gotten away with it too many times already. The Sheriff had been watching you; I noticed that while I stayed around the area. I was haunting you, staying as close as I could, despite calls from the other side to come through. I was determined not to leave until you had paid for what you did. I took the Sheriff and carried out your sentence. Did you really think you were the only one capable of figuring out it could be done?" Sneering at his solid form like he was a child playing with toys. "I was just quicker than you, eighty years quicker. Anger accomplishes many things."

Silence, followed by a strange wailing noise and then she became the dark mist once again. The whispering of many voices joined hers before she regained control. "I was alright for a long time after that, watching you wander around in the nothing. I enjoyed that. But then she came along and gave you a way back in. I couldn't allow that to continue."

Neither spirit noticed me as they engaged in a struggle long coming. I was free for the moment but wasn't so sure Sierra wouldn't come back for a second try at my living body. For five seconds, I had been sympathetic towards her, about the time she made me experience her death. But as time progressed, I was quickly getting over that along with any pity I'd ever had for Perry-James, whoever he was. I was just angry now. Angry and just as unsubstantial as they were for the moment. I didn't care that she was a murder victim and he the murderer. They were both completely evil jackasses and I was going to make them leave.

I watched the teenager have an animated conversation with the black mist and decided it was best to act while they were distracted. With an instinct to save both living people in this messed up reunion, me being one of them, I did something stupid. Taking a deep breath, I joined the party. Poor nameless guy was already crowded full of James, but I went in anyway, with no idea how to do it, and technically not be a dead person. It was the weirdest experience I'd ever had; and that was saying something because, well, look at what I'd been through so far.

In an instant, I was breathing through someone else's lungs, looking at hands that weren't mine and competing for space with a soul who thought he'd figured it all out. Well, he was wrong. James had been so involved in arguing with the woman who'd cheated him out of his life, ignoring the fact that he had done the same to her before that; my presence caught him by surprise. He felt like an oily spot on this kid's otherwise clean feeling aura, soiling it with the wrongness of his presence. He was where he should not be, causing all kinds of harm to his helpless victim. Heart rate was too fast, blood pressure too high; the human body wasn't designed to carry more than one soul at a time, and this one was sucking up all his energy. I felt this young man's pain and knew my presence was making it worse. Unnamed kid was too crowded; James had pushed him so far into his head, he barely knew what was happening. He was a virtual zombie about to have a heart attack under the stress of carrying two, now three souls. Thinking he had total control, James hadn't expected a confrontation in his temporary home. I had to work quickly, using that element of surprise to my advantage. For the moment, we were of equal substance, he and I. I was connecting with him on a level I couldn't before.

Reminding myself I couldn't stay this way forever; I really did have a living body to return to, I took hold of James's energy, hoping with all my heart this worked the way I wanted it to.

Take back over, kid, I'm trying to save you. I spoke to the boy within his own head. A swift intake of breath shared by three entities; me, James, and the kid, and with a force powered by desperation, we shoved his slimy essence out, mine following close behind. The kid immediately fell to the ground, his body hitting hard enough to make dirt fly upward. Giving him a chance to recover his senses, I stayed a filmy specter facing Sierra and James in a world that looked slightly out of focus and felt further away than it had before.

"What are you doing?" James was angry and fully focused on me and what I had just done, forgetting the poor guy lying on the ground like a carelessly dropped toy.

"You need to leave," I said firmly, trying to maintain a strong confident front, despite a growing unease about my unattended body just yards away. I was distressingly aware of Sierra looming close to me, hoping it didn't occur to her I was an open husk, ripe for re-infestation. "You're killing him," I added, hoping James's death had given him a conscience despite all he had done while alive. You know, the whole spiritual healing thing that occurs when you connect with the great beyond.

"You're speaking as if I care," he said. Now here was the real James. I felt that strongly as the last pretense of charming, nice guy slowly slipped away. A slight pause followed as if he realized what he had said, and a last attempt to regain his Mr. Nice Guy status. "He will be fine Maddie." I wasn't convinced he meant that.

"You're a killer," Sierra and I said together as if we still shared a common body.

"No, I was a good man," he said. This last time his voice was low and hard to hear as if even he didn't quite hold that conviction. "I made the world better without them." Crickets chirped all around us, the sound getting louder as all conversation ceased.

I think we all knew this discussion was useless.

Looking down at the fallen boy, I knew James couldn't be allowed to go back in there, and I'll be damned if the only other body available in this area was going to accept either of these things into it. Trying not to give my thoughts away, I started to drift from the two spirits with the full

169

intention of getting to myself first. But was stopped before I started by the idea that I was leaving the kid at their mercy, lying on the ground, a helpless victim. Damn it! What was I going to do? I had made all this effort, without really solving the problem. It was still human vs ghosts, and they could move in and start it all again. I had to act fast, but wasn't sure what to do next. In the end, the issue was settled without my having to do a thing.

"I could have done so much more," handsome, charming manners still intact, the madman who'd occupied so much of my time continued to speak, moving toward his former shell to take possession once again, not caring that the boy couldn't take much more of his abuse. "You took that from me so I guess it's fitting that I took care of you first." At last, the admission of guilt Sierra had been waiting for. Too bad it was accompanied by his habitual excuses to spoil the moment. "But you made me do it, showing me that you were just like them. I had no choice."

I guess that last statement was too much for Sierra. Her lovely gray form began to grow dark, becoming that black mist again. Only this time, she wasn't alone, I counted seven other misty entities moving in toward James's gray form, his face showing disbelief at first, then horror, as all his victims joined with her to converge upon him. Sounds unlike I'd ever heard before came from the murky mess as my own anchorless soul rushed back to my fleshy form.

Chapter Forty-One-Maddie

He's gone; I haven't seen or heard from James for almost a year. I'm sure that his victims took their revenge, making him face what he had done to them. From what I could recall, his last minutes were full of horrid noises coming from the large black mass surrounding him. Whatever they were doing to him on their level must have been bad. I was more worried about getting back to my body at that point and was less interested in what was happening to a soul I was sure needed disposing of. Slipping back in was traumatic enough that I was sure I wouldn't be trying this kind of thing again for quite some time, if ever. Nauseated, with a headache from hell, I returned to a body bruised and bloody from the thorn bushes. Wanting nothing more than to lie there and puke, I forced myself to move; that kid was still out there in the middle of all that activity. While I would have rather just crawled out and headed to my car, I scraped together some extra courage and decided to go to the rescue of the only other living person in the area.

I freed myself from the brambles and made it to the guy's side. When I got there, I was relieved to find all was quiet. He was alone, waking up and terrified. He knew who I was, having seen me at the hotel but wasn't sure how we both wound up where we were. I came up with a lame story of my getting lost and his driving up and coming to my rescue before slipping on a puddle and falling on the ground. He chose to accept this story as true, blankly nodding his head as I expressed concern over his fall and thanked him profusely for helping me out of the woods. I was a crappy liar and we both knew it, but anything else was too weird to consider. So, we made it to our separate cars, still numb over the events we'd just experienced, and drove back to the hotel, never to see each other again, though I learned he called in sick one day and quit a few days after that. I stayed on at the hotel for a week longer, on high alert for any type of contact from James or Sierra but nothing happened. I slept better than I ever had, no dreams or any tingling of my ghostly sensors. Life was like it had been before; well, except for being unemployed, living in a hotel and having spiritual PTSD. I could have let it end there, walked off and taken up where I left off in life, but I had the strange sensation there was one bit of unfinished business I needed to tend to.

Driving once again to the scene of James's death, I made my way back to his abandoned truck. It was just as it had been when I saw it last, rusted door partially open, moldy fingers strewn across the seat. I.D cards with the names of all his victims written on them. Carefully gathering the evidence of his crime together and placing them in the bag, I searched the interior for proof of ownership, anything I could use to identify the owner. The glove compartment seemed a logical place to look. It popped open with an ease I hadn't expected from being closed for so long and revealed everything I needed. Not only did I find his registration and driver's identification card, I also found two more faded identity papers for women not acknowledged on Sheriff Richardson's list and a neatly folded tourist map for the park as it was in the 1930's. I sat there in the bright sunlight looking at the clearly marked trails among the standard markings for mountains and wooded areas. And low and behold there they were, ten small dots placed in a circle just beyond a central hiking route. Apparently, he wanted to make sure he kept them all together and didn't trust his memory to find his way back to the exact spot he'd chosen. And beneath it all, the icing on the cake, a small notebook, names and dates, along with details on how he had rid the world of them in neat, easy to read print. Bingo! I was happy more for the other nine women than for Sierra at this moment. They were going to get closure from somewhere. He was going to have to take responsibility for what he'd done. I knew he was dead, but somewhere he had to be aware he was going to be front page news for what he had done, he was not a good guy and the world would know it.

Thinking of this as only a person who watches television crime shows can, I tried not to move things too much, restoring them to the spot I'd known them to be in the other night when I'd been here under different circumstances, after taking pictures of it all, of course. Dave was going to have a field day with this, I thought as I exited the truck, placing as quick call to the Sheriff's office to report what I'd just stumbled across.

I only had to wait twenty minutes for the officers to arrive. There was no great crime wave going on here and my find had piqued their interest. I played it well, avid hiker finds abandoned truck just off the trail with a bunch of incriminating evidence of a serial killer lying right there for over eighty years. I answered their questions, though they didn't ask many. They weren't interested in me, more in what they found and how it would look in the news. With a satisfied sigh, I walked back to my car, leaving this all behind. I remember, just for a second, that slight panicked feeling of a familiar presence in the air, as if I were being studied closely. It couldn't be! James was gone, our connection severed. I would have known if he had come back. I felt his absence like a welcome void I had no interest in filling. The feeling lasted for such a short time in which I studied my surroundings with dread, like a war-weary soldier ready to fight again to stay alive. Then, seeing the deer standing on the path, looking at me with guarded interest, let out a sigh of relief, laughed it off, and drove away.

James's story made headlines and I let Dave take all the credit for that, sending him everything as soon as I returned to my hotel room. Not caring about how this played out from now on. I just wanted to start my life again. I packed up and left the hotel for good later that day. It was over, and I intended to put it all behind me.

I don't talk to many dead people anymore. It's too hard to deal with most of them, they carry problems with them even after death. Though I am better at protecting myself than I used to be. I had experienced enough of the bad stuff to curb my enthusiasm for the supernatural. If I can't fix it by talking them through it, they are talking to the wrong sensitive person. I am strong enough to make them leave when I want them to. I have a good job now, the same company who'd hired me before gave me another chance and I'm doing well. I live in a nice house, have good friends, and made up with Damen who has forgiven me enough to visit frequently. It took me a while to bring it in to the conversation, but I had shared a little of my life after death experience, leaving out the most extreme stuff. He had been quite understanding and willing to listen, I took that as a good sign. It hadn't scared him off and we progressed to the next level. Sex was great without an audience!

I'm no longer interested in ghost hunter programs or scary movies. Firsthand experience with the subject matter has made me appreciate life and the living of it. I write this out, to be seen by no-one while I'm still alive, just as a recollection of events as I lived them to be put up and visited later. Having said all this, I'm slipping this into a folder and going on a date tonight, just me and Damen, no dead company welcome.

Epilogue

I was not a good man; I can see that now. That last evening spent with Maddie brought it all back to me. What I had done was savage and yet more satisfying than all the other things I'd done in my life, even loving Sierra. That love was a lie; I see it clearly now. Sierra was faithless, causing her own death; I had wasted years worshipping her. What she and the others did to me during our last encounter was horrible. Those women pulled me into the nothing, trying to force me to the light. It flared up with the intention to take me and make me answer for my actions while I was alive. I felt it waiting to take me, but understood that in order to gain forgiveness, I would have to answer for all I had done to them; I wasn't about to do that. I knew what I had done. All memory had returned, along with the feeling of justification for my actions. I don't know how long I was trapped with those women. But, despite all their best efforts, making me relive their deaths, sharing what they felt during the end of their lives, their anger at being taken from life too soon, telling me I had no right to do what I had done; I was untouched by any guilt or remorse. All I could focus on was the fact it had all ended for me long before it should have. I should have had more time to clean up this world. Though, I must say, I was no longer of the opinion that blonde women were nasty and bad. This encounter just clarified for me that all women were bad, capable of turning on men as quickly as a cobra on a mouse. Oh, yes, all women, especially Maddie. I had trusted her to guide me through my confusion but she had led me to them, even allowing herself to be used by Sierra to confront me. Together these women managed to distract me and free a chosen vehicle from my control, attacking me like a helpless boy. I didn't like it. They were acting as if I should care about them, about what I had done, hoping I would cry and ask for forgiveness for everything. Trouble was, I really didn't care, and forgiveness was the last thing I wanted. It was quite easy to adjust to what I was, once I admitted what I wanted. The only thing that bothered me was that it had taken this long to remember it all. When I finally freed myself from their annoying, pathetic presences, letting the light take them into its warmth; I felt so liberated. Turns out, after I failed to show remorse, the light didn't want me, after all. Moving as far away as I could, I watched it take them. The experience had taught me a valuable thing; all women were to be despised. I understood this quite well now. Armed with this new perspective, I was able to follow that thin trail, with great difficulty but a determination that made it possible nonetheless, back to Maddie's window. Whereas before I would have contacted her as soon as I could, I hung back, finding a body among the policemen wandering around my truck. I picked a young, healthy one who had been assigned to block off what was now considered a crime scene. Stupid, really, they would never be able to do anything to me now, but they had to go through the motions of an investigation. Pleading the need to pee, I left my fellow officers and wandered a little further into the forest. That's when I saw her, Maddie was walking toward her car, a satisfied look on her traitorous face. I wanted to use this body to make her pay for what she had done, but something held me back, I just stood there and stared. Seeing her brought back so many emotions and I guess old habits showed through. For just a second, my soul sought our old connection; her head shot up and she looked about cautiously. Remembering our last encounter in which she surprised me by using her spirit to push me out of the boy, I decided now was not the time to let that happen again. Turning quickly, I moved back into the woods, leaving her to think I was truly gone. I heard her car engine start. She drove off and I stayed in my new flesh home for a while, blending in with the living long enough to catch a ride back into town. It's been over a year now since I decided this world was a better place for me than the dead place. I have occupied many bodies during that time. They seem to wear out so quickly. I choose carefully, mostly young people or those with strong constitutions. I've gotten so good at it, I can smell any weakness that might make them unsuitable. My work has continued in different cities, different victims; it's quite wonderful because I can't be caught. I use a different body every time, so they can never connect a single person to the missing women. Maddie has no clue I'm still around; she's moved on. I am aware that spirits visit her; she is a well-known beacon to the many lost souls I encounter moving through the living world. I can hear them now and again, in passing. Our contact is brief. I'm not like them at all. I live. Moving around so much, I don't want to forget what I've been up to. I have to keep a running tally; so, I keep a diary, leaving it in a place I can always get to when I've found a new shell. I can read it and add the trophies I've collected for my own satisfaction. As I think of it now, I can't help but smile through my borrowed flesh, smearing the lipstick from its thin lips and looking at the pale made up face in the mirror. I'd never used one of their own against them before. This should be fun. She speaks aloud as I tell her what to write, and we both think of Maddie again. Let her get comfortable with my absence. wondering if I should pay her a visit when she least expects me. I'd really enjoy that. After all, I have all the time in the world.

The End

www.ingramcontent.com/pod-product-compliance
Lightning Source LLC
Chambersburg PA
CBHW071518170626
46811CB00007B/2898